IMAGES

Expressive Moments From The Mind's Eye

To Kent —
Edward Gilliam
1/18/94

CLOUDS REST PUBLISHING
PARIS, ILLINOIS

Succulent

IMAGES

Expressive Moments From The Mind's Eye

EDWARD GILLUM

I M A G E S

Expressive Moments From The Mind's Eye

LIBRARY OF CONGRESS CATALOG CARD NUMBER 93-090293
INTERNATIONAL STANDARD BOOK NUMBER 0-912705-01-9

Edward Gillum 1938-
Edward Gillum
Photography, Artistic

First Printing 1993

Printing: Dai Nippon, Japan

CLOUDS REST PUBLISHING
Paris, Illinois

Dedicated to
Ansel Adams

The artistry of Ansel Adams began as
a child when he touched the keys of a piano for the first time.
Ansel learned how to make beautiful sounds to the ear,
then through his infinite talents, he transferred those
same sounds to the mind's eye in his photographs.
If a camera can be melodic, he certainly
had the formula to fine tune it.
The rigorous discipline associated with his music is
evident in his several thousand expressive negatives.
Ansel's contribution to the fine art of
photography is equaled only by his contribution
to his fellow photographers.
He taught us all how to see with the camera in a
very special way. Those of us who were privileged to have
known Ansel were indeed fortunate to have shared
in his extraordinary knowledge of craft.
It is with profound appreciation that I dedicate
this body of work.

CONTENTS

Introduction

When I began black-and-white photography in the 1970's, I wasn't aware of visualization and its importance in rendering a fine art concept. Visualization can only come with considerable experience in the photographic medium.

I began a career in commercial art in the 1950's, and for anyone who has experienced design and production in art, they too have had to visualize the end result of the project. I have always been a firm believer that the creative mind is present at birth, and that it develops and grows with ambitious encouragement. I do not believe photography, like art, can be taught to the extent of perfection without natural born talent. Photographers, like artists, are born, not created in schools. A photographer cannot be taught how to compose or visualize an image. Only technique can be taught. One can be taught all of the fundamentals of music and the piano, and they may become a good piano player, but not a concert pianist of renowned quality, without born ability, creative ambition and talent.

In commercial art, I was always able to visualize the final work from ideas put forth by other artists or clients. I have always been able to see art or a photographic subject in my mind's eye in color without any hesitation. This is natural self-training. However, visualization of a subject in color and transferring the hues to shades of black, gray tones, and whites was not an easy feat for me in my earlier days of black-and-white photography.

The best training in visualization is continual practice in darkroom printing. From this will come retention of the gray values, which when in the field will be recalled and applied to new subjects and situations. Our visualization will be enhanced when a good knowledge of filters and their application is exercised. We must be able to visualize separation of tones, and then know which filter, exposure and development will guarantee the desired results.

The Zone System and visualization go hand-in-hand. With proper visualization of the subject, and application of the Zone System, all the tones print with exacting accuracy. Then, the fine art photographer becomes expressive through the camera, creating expressive moments from the mind's eye.

Throughout this chronicle of photographic images, I have tried to be as accurate as possible in detailing technique of craft. I have kept good records of film, lenses, filters, exposures and development procedures of important negatives throughout my years with the camera. It is not easy, however, to keep detailed information regarding the position of the camera and adjustments, such as swings and tilts of front and rear standards. I can look at a print, and with reasonable accuracy, analyze the supposed adjustments I made at the time of exposure.

Good photography is creative imagination. We do not see the image in a literal or realistic sense. We do not make a factual record of the subject, but an interpretive rendering. My intent is to draw the viewer into the subject with the realization of form and light. Vision then becomes reality.

—*Edward Gillum*

Oak Canyon Creek, Morning Light
Anaheim, California

After going through one rain storm after another, I decided to take advantage of one fine, warm California sunny day in the middle of February. I had not had an opportunity to make any new photographs for several weeks, and welcomed a chance to explore nearby areas.

I packed up my 4x5 view camera and headed for Oak Canyon Park, a beautiful and remote wilderness area nestled in the rural foothills of Anaheim.

The early morning light was soft and quite enveloping when I arrived at the park just after sunrise. It was apparent that I had at least an hour before the sun would rise over the nearby hills.

When I came upon this subject–Oak Canyon Creek–I immediately saw the final print in my mind's eye. The sun, rising over a nearby hill, began to shine on the trunk and upper limb of the old and shapely oak tree. The highlights accented its form, separating it from the background foliage. The scene was quite flat otherwise, so I knew reduced exposure and expanded development was necessary to give the subject depth. The muddy water in the creek–actually pumped runoff from the soaked hills– was flat and lacking in substance and important detail. Using a 240 Nikkor lens at f/64 with the shutter set for a time exposure of 6 seconds I created a softness to the slow moving water. My film was HP5+ rated at a speed of ASA 260. Normal plus development was in Pyro.

There is sharp detail and resolution in the negative, which prints well on grade 2 Arista glossy fiber base paper. Only a slight edge burn is give to the right side to bring it into balance with the other areas of the image. Toning is in Selenium (1:12 in hypo clearing agent) for 7 minutes. Although the final print before toning has good substance, there is a remarkable increase in density and brilliance to this image after toning.

This scene had a wonderful mood and feeling, even though rather flat in reality.

Sky Feathers at Sunrise
Bodie, California

The high desert near Bodie is desolate and true to the western landscape. The road is rough and bumpy and considerable time is spent driving from Lee Vining, on the Eastern Sierra, to this ghost town of yesteryear.

It was rather cold in the early morning October sun. There were ponds with thin coatings of ice. A strong wind was blowing, creating many rapidly changing cloud designs against the dark blue sky. In my visualization of this subject, I saw a strong, almost silhouetted mountain range slightly highlighted against a dark sky. The effect was to show the clouds and their feathered structure as the dominating part of the image. I was facing south and the strong bright sun was coming from the left, shimmering across the lower surfaces of the clouds.

I set up my 8 x 10 view camera with a 9 1/4-inch Nikkor lens. This was my primary lens of the time for the 8 x 10. I can recall how many beautiful and different compositions came and went while I was setting up my camera. With the camera positioned and the scene composed against the mountains, I waited for the right cloud formation. Using my spot meter, I took various readings. The mountain range was the darkest and was placed on Zone IV. The deep No. 25 red filter in combination with a polarizing filter lowered the darkest parts to Zone II or below. The sky fell between Zones V/VI and the brightest parts of the clouds on VII. The basic exposure was f/11 at 1/250 second, however, the filter factors called for a plus 4 1/3 stops. The adjusted exposure was f 8/11 at 1/15 second. To keep the early morning values of the cloud highlights between Zones VII and VIII, I indicated Normal-plus-one development in HC-110 (1:7) for the Tri-X film at ASA 200.

The print is on Elite grade 4 developed two minutes in Edwal Ultra Black (1:7), with benzotriazole added to brighten the high values. Using a card with a hole in it, I burn the top cloud area back and forth for 200 percent of the basic exposure.

Cloud patterns and their designs—known as nephograms—have always been exciting to photograph. Once the shutter is tripped, capturing a second of time, no exact duplication is ever possible.

Granite Wall and the Kings River
Kings Canyon National Park

The Sierra Nevada is one of the most magnificent mountain ranges in the world. It extends 400 miles from south to north and is basically a huge, single block that has been elevated by a tremendous upper force, and then tilted by fault action from east to west, gradually sloping on the west and with more than a 12,000-foot vertical wall on the east.

Carved through sheer granite is the Kings Canyon, one of nature's most rugged and majestic regions. I have photographed numerous locations of great granite displays, but none compare with this area of the Sierra.

I had spent two days hiking, exploring and photographing Tokopah Falls near the Kaweah River west of Lodgepole at the southern extremity; and Roaring River Falls near the Kings River to the north.

On the third day, I was up before dawn and was driving west from Cedar Grove along the Kings River. I stopped the car and began walking along the river's edge. A tremendous display of granite glistened in the early morning light. The river rapids were quite violent as they surged past me. I set up my tripod and 4 x 5 field camera on a solid area at the rocky edge of the river. I was able to visualize the final photograph of the subject before me. I saw an image of a great granite wall of fine sharpness and detail, in contrast to the soft, rapidly moving flow of the river a few feet below.

The sun was not yet above the mountain tops, but the light reflecting from the upper atmosphere gave almost a silvery highlight to the mist covered granite. Using a 7 1/4-inch Schneider Symmar S lens, I made the exposure on Agfapan 100 using a speed of ASA 64. To show considerable movement of the water I used a 1/2 second exposure; and because of the early morning low light, I had to settle for an f stop of 5.6.

The shadows of the granite wall were quite pronounced and placed on Zone III. With very good detail to the water, the highlights were placed on Zone VII, and no filter was used. The negative was given Normal development in FG7 with a 1:15 dilution and a little sodium sulfite added. Early prints were made on Ilfobrom grade 2 developed 2 minutes in Edwal Ultra Black (1:7). I have found recently that I have made improved prints of a greater silver brilliancy and depth using Arista Classic grade 2, giving slightly less exposure and developing the print in Glycin 130 (1:1), and extending toning in selenium to 6 minutes. I have also made excellent prints on Galerie grade 2.

Using a card, there is an additional 20 percent burn-in of the water from the granite down to the bottom.

I have marveled at the many great walls and cliffs of the Kings Canyon region, and never tire of exploring for new photographic subjects.

Ascending Boulder, Alabama Hills
Owens Valley, California

The Owens Valley is faced by the Eastern Sierra range which extends nearly 400 miles north to south. Mount Whitney dominates this vast region which consists of 14,000-foot walls of granite and rugged gorges. The Owens Valley is a basin lying between this vast Sierra range and the White Mountains and Inyo Range. At the turn of the century, farming and cattle ranching in the area of Lone Pine was very productive. The land was rich and lush with an abundance of water until aqueducts were put in to divert the water south to the growing Los Angeles area. The soil eroded and farming came to a halt in the region. As the ground dried up, so did the quaint small towns in the Owens Valley–with the exception of Bishop, the only real thriving community today.

Running parallel to the Sierra is a string of small towns, from Olancha at the southern end to Bridgeport at the northern. Lone Pine, where many western movies have been filmed over the last 50 years, sits at the foot of Mount Whitney. Bordering the west and northwest of Lone Pine is a mass of weather-beaten, wind-eroded rock formations of all shapes and sizes. Desolate and dry much of the year–certainly a region unto its own–the area still emits greatness and beauty. The shapes, sizes and designs of the rock formations are very impressive and highly photogenic.

One winter day I had been driving up at the higher altitude near the Whitney portal. It was dry, windy and cold with considerable haze and smoke from a local fire in the foothills below Whitney. I decided to go back down near the Alabama Hills and away from the air pollutants.

Arriving back in the basin, I set up my 4 x 5 view camera at a location I felt best for photographing formations I had seen earlier that day. It was mid-afternoon–the sunlight was soft due to thin high clouds and smoke, but the shadows were good. My lens was a 7 1/4-inch Schneider Symmar S–an extremely sharp lens of high resolution. The film was Super XX 200 (rated at ASA 100). The luminous scale of 6 1/2 Zones was higher than anticipated, and quite expansive even though the sun was somewhat subdued. I placed the dark crevices of the boulder low between Zones II/III. The blue sky fell between Zones VI/VII–the brightest part of the sunny side of the boulder fell on VII and the white cloud highlights on Zone VIII. The exposure was 1/4 second at f/ 32/45. The negative was developed in ABC Pyro for 6 minutes. The print was made on Mitsubishi grade 4 developed in LPD (1:3) for 2 minutes followed by toning in selenium for 6 minutes. After experimenting with various print values at the high end of the scale, I determined there to be more solidity to this image when printed slightly darker (about one Zone) for the sky, clouds and left side of the boulder. This requires an additional burn of 30 percent of the basic exposure using a card with a hole in it.

Owens River at Dawn
Lone Pine, California

The unparalleled beauty of the Owens Valley lies on the east side of the Sierra from Olancha to Bishop, California. To the west, running nearly 70 unbroken miles, is the spectacular Southern Sierra range, cresting with Mount Whitney, the highest peak in the continental United States, at 14,496 feet. To the east are the much older Inyo and White Mountains.

The picturesque majesty of the Palisade Crest is forever changing with each passing hour of the sun's movement. Ice carved gorges, windswept granite and jagged peaks add mystery and splendor in all seasons. John Muir thought the Sierra range was the most divinely beautiful of any mountain-chain he had ever seen. He remarked of "great flooded light shining on silvery icy peaks, and the flush of noonday radiance on the trees, rocks and snow." Exploring the Owens Valley gives new meaning and satisfaction to what composes the human spirit.

On one particular trip to the valley, I had driven east from the main road in Lone Pine to the Lone Pine station. From this area there is an awe-inspiring view of Lone Pine Peak and the Alabama Hills nestled in front of this towering mountain range.

It was nearly five in the morning. Dawn was just starting to break. The sun had not yet risen over the White Mountains to the east. I have visited this part of the Valley many times before, and had crossed the Owens River each time, but had not seen the stillness and the reflections that were evident on this particular morning. The reflections were of a silvery/gray quality. I explored the banks of the river on both sides, composing with a framing card, and visualizing numerous images of the final print. I set up my tripod on the west bank, facing to the east and into the blue sky of dawn. The reflections were quite pronounced at this angle. With my spot meter, I took numerous readings of the subject. The darkest areas were of the reflected tree trunks – placed between Zones II and III. The tree trunks above the water fell on Zone IV, and the gray water on IV/V. The brightest areas of the scene were of the sky's reflection in the water – up around Zone VII/VIII. I used 4x5 Tri-X film rated at 260. Using a 12-inch lens, I gave an exposure of 1/8 second at f 22/32. Development was Normal in PMK Pyro for 11 minutes. The print, on Arista Classic grade 2, is toned in Selenium for 8 minutes. The light, while not noticeable at the time of exposure, was greater on the right side. The print therefore requires an additional edge-burn of about 20 percent of the basic exposure.

Snow, Stick and Ice Patches
Hesperia, California

I had spent all morning in the Big Bear area of Southern California photographing remnants of a recent snow. The sun was warm and the air clear at the high altitude. I drove many of the back roads taking advantage of the fine, crisp winter day.

Many of the dried buds from fall were still on the desert plants. Snow-capped and hidden in the morning shade, they now glistened as the sun began to shine over a nearby ridge.

I was driving near Hesperia, not far from Big Bear, but at a lower altitude. Snow was melting rapidly. I parked the car and walked along the old road, looking at the sparkle of the wet snow on some of the thistles. There was snowmelt at the bank of the ditch, and below, a dead stick protruding from ice patches. I immediately visualized the photograph, its darks, mid-tones and highlights, in my mind's eye. The image, which I saw as rather stylized, was exciting. With a black card with a 4 x 5 opening in it, I composed the subject which fit well into the horizontal format. I set up the wooden tripod with my 4 x 5 field camera and a 7 1/4-inch Schneider Symmar S lens. Taking numerous readings with my spot meter, I placed the darkest part of the ice on Zone III. The lightest part of the ice fell on Zone V; the sun on the edge of the stick on VI. Although the snow was at an angle on the bank and in shade, it fell 1/2 zone higher (between VI/VII) than the sun on the stick.

The image shown here was made on Tri-X (at ASA 120) for one second at f 45. Development was Normal plus-one in HC-110 (1:7) for 8 1/2 minutes. I made three other shorter exposures on Tri-X (at ASA 160), all developed normally in various solutions of D-23 followed by Kodalk; and D-23 using the water bath technique, but the first exposure held more detail and expanded the tones in a more acceptable manner.

I have had very good results printing this image on Galerie grade 2 developed in Edwal Ultra Black with a little potassium bromide added, and on Mitsubushi grade 3 in Selectol Soft (1:1) 1 1/2 minutes followed by LPD (1:3) 1 minute. Toning is in selenium (1:20) for 8 minutes.

Forest in Winter Light
Wrightwood, California

A wonderful and quaint village known as Wrightwood, sits at the foothills of the San Gabriel Mountains in the Angeles National Forest in California. In summer, Wrightwood enjoys warm temperatures, cool breezes and a peaceful atmosphere. During most winters it is blanketed with snow and enjoys a thriving ski and recreational business.

A monument to the beauty of Southern California is Mount San Antonio–referred to locally as Old Baldy–a peak with an altitude of over 10,000 feet.

Photographing dozens of times in the area, I always find new and exciting images every time I explore around Wrightwood. The terrain below Wrightwood is rich with the beauty of dry desert scrub among granite rocks, boulders and sheer walls. Higher altitudes, near the village, are thick with forests and lush meadows.

It was a mild winter day when I drove the old road west of Wrightwood, down past Jackson Lake to a forest of fir pines and sequoias. I had stopped along this road many times and had made numerous photographs of pine cones, tree detail and reeds around the lake shoreline. On this afternoon, the scene was particularly serene. The sun was warm and the lighting soft and enveloping. I parked my car along an old dirt road and carried my equipment to a spot that was quite visually impressive. I was using my Wista 4 x 5 field camera of cherry wood construction. Many of my earlier photographs were made with an Omega monorail view camera of metal design, considerably heavier to pack on long hikes. The Wista, being lighter and smaller, makes hiking and back-packing much easier.

I removed a framing card from my case (a card with a 4 x 5 hole cut in it for viewing a composition). I immediately saw the composition of the Forest in Winter Light and visualized the final black-and-white image in my mind's eye. I first saw the image as horizontal, but as I turned the framing card vertically, I realized it was a more appealing view of the subject. With my spot meter I took several readings of the subjects light values. The darkest, shaded side of the largest tree was placed between Zones II/III. The shadow on the ground was on Zone III and the green boughs between III/IV. The bright highlights at the rear of the scene fell on Zone VII–not of such extreme brightness, but I knew the values would be closer to Zone VIII because of the light at the high altitude. I also knew the exposure range would be about six Zones (or f stops). My lens, a 7 1/4-inch Schneider Symmar S of extremely sharp quality, was set at f 32 for 1/8 second for the exposure on Super XX film (rated at ASA 160. In order to hold all of the detail in the high values, I indicated Normal development in ABC Pyro with continuous agitation. I made a few duplicate negatives which were developed in D-23, however, the one in the Pyro–which almost always produces yellow stains and adds considerable density–was very sharp with high acutance.

I have always found back-lighted subjects such as this to be quite natural and expressive of the fine print. For me, the viewing of this print represents the actual visualized image that I saw at the time of exposure.

Sunset at Point Sur
Point Sur, California

I had spent the day in the Carmel area looking for subjects to photograph. Much of the time was in Carmel Valley, a beautiful country setting which displays the true California ranching and farming community. This particular day was quite hazy though. I had seen several good compositions, but nothing that left me excited. The harsh light hampered the situation during the mid-day.

In early afternoon, I decided to drive to Carmel Highlands to see Virginia Adams. Virginia, gracious as she always is, was most agreeable to talking of Ansel and many of their experiences over the years. We discussed our previous times and workshops together. Ansel's work is still very much evident. His darkroom is intact and his hundreds of books and photographs are throughout the house.

After our most cordial visit, I headed south on highway 101 toward San Luis Obispo county. As I came upon Big Sur a beautiful sunset was taking place. I hurried to set up my 4x5 view camera about 75 feet from the road, at an area overlooking sand and desert scrub. As the sun lowered closer to the horizon, a misty fog began to form at the base of Point Sur. It was getting quite dark. I was hoping for sufficient light to remain on the foreground as the sun began to dip into the sea.

At first I considered using a filter to bring out the subtle clouds in the sky, but I realized a filter would darken the shadow area of the foreground too much, possibly even to the deadness of black.

The dark shadows were placed between Zones I/II. The sky fell on Zone VIII. The sun, still extremely bright, fell high on the scale to the equivalent of Zone XI. I made two exposures on Tri-X at ASA 300. One exposure was 1/8 second at F 22, the other at 1/2 second. The foreground in the 1/8 second negative was far too dark. The 1/2 second exposure was correct showing fine detail in the brush.

These two exposures, the only ones made that day, left me very unexcited and disenchanted with this particular trip.

After returning home, I placed the film holder in a "baggy" on the shelf in the darkroom. I had forgotten they were there during all the times I was processing other negatives. It was nearly two years later that I decided to develop them. The film was now out of date, and I fully expected some fogging to occur. I could still remember the bright sun and scene at the time of exposure. To hold all of the high values, I decided to develop the negatives in Pyro (PMK) at Normal minus one. When I saw the negatives in the hypo, I was quite pleased with the detail in them. And so, too, it has been gratifying to make large prints of this image. I am glad that I did not pull the slide and discard the film before processing, as I had thought of doing many times. The print, on Arista Classic fiber base paper, was developed in Glycin 130, 1:1 for 3 minutes. There is a considerable amount of burning required in the making of this print. The basic exposure is 42 seconds. After the first 12 seconds of exposure, I dodge (or cover) the lower 2/3 from just above the fog line to the bottom of the image. Using a card with a hole in it, and working in a circular motion, I burn in the sun and the top right corner section from the horizon on upward to the top edge for an additional 35 seconds. To intensify the image and give it an overall richness, the print is toned in a selenium/hypo clearing agent solution (1:12) for 6 minutes.

Fir Trees and Winter Storm
Yosemite National Park

All of my days spent in Yosemite National Park have been experiences of immeasurable grandeur. To me the western slope of the Sierra Nevada is the most beautiful of any place that I have ever been. For those who have never had the great pleasure of walking the trails to Yosemite Falls, or strolling meadows smelling of summer grass and wildflowers, its beauty is beyond their richest dreams. Not only is the valley itself filled with spectacular sights, the entire 1200 square miles of Yosemite are magnificent all times of the year.

The rocky area of Tenaya Lake and the fragrant wildflowers in spring in Tuolumne Meadows are proof of the diversity of this grand monument to nature.

I have developed a tremendous love of the area over the many years that I have visited and photographed Yosemite. Each new visit is filled with the excitement and wonder of all the times of the past years. The bold domineering cliffs of granite and lofty waterfalls fill the soul with inspiration and appreciation for the natural beauty of the earth. A winter's day can be mild and sunny, or cold and dramatic with violent snow storms.

One January day in 1980, I arrived at the lodge at El Portal. The temperature was mild and the sky overcast with gray lifeless clouds. I had explored the valley late in the evening, but disenchanted with the flat light and discouraged by the drizzly weather, I decided to return to the lodge for the night.

When I arose the next morning, there was a light rain falling. I was aware that the lodge was of lower altitude than Yosemite Valley, and the colder temperature almost assured me of snow at a higher elevation.

When I arrived in the valley, the view was spectacular. I spent the entire day virtually all alone, photographing many glorious subjects in the falling snow. When the image, Fir Trees and Winter Storm, was made in early afternoon, the snow had begun to turn to drizzle and was extremely wet. I made this image with a 35mm Nikon and 2-inch lens on Tri-X film. Visually, the negative appears somewhat soft, but it prints well on grade 3 paper. I did not keep records of 35mm exposures at the time, but judge the development to have been normal.

Early prints were on grade 4 paper through a fairly heavy diffusion filter. I had not made any other prints since then, until experimenting with the negative when making prints for this book. I discovered recently that there is considerably more detail and information in the negative than I had previously realized. The basic exposure is 23 seconds at f 8. The three sections of dark trees at the right one third are dodged up and down for 7 seconds each to hold back the dark tones at the point of separation. With a hole in a card, a burn-in of 7 seconds is given to the faint background trees at both left and right sides of the dark tree trunks. There is a very minimum of detail to the snow at the very base of the print. Using a card, I burn-in the bottom white area for 60 seconds.

The print, on Mitsubishi grade 3, is developed in Selectol Soft (1:1) 1 minute, followed by 2 minutes in Edwal Ultra Black (1:7). Toning is in selenium (1:20) for 9 minutes.

Jeffrey Pine at Sunrise, Sentinel Dome
Yosemite National Park, California

I have had the good fortune to visit and photograph in Yosemite National Park many, many times over the years. Each season brings new and glorious images for the photographer. No matter where one turns, there is always a subject—in summer, soft moods exist in meadows graced with wildflowers—in winter, violent storms create dramatic compositions of chiseled granite covered with clouds and an abundance of ice and snow.

Meadows I photographed in the warm sun of June, have on occasion become blanketed with snow during one of nature's surprises on the Fourth of July. The weather in the Sierra is very unpredictable at all times of the year.

On one warm spring day I was up at sunrise, and with my car packed, headed for Glacier Point by way of Badger Pass. With me I had my 4 x 5 Omega view camera, two lenses, various filters, film holders and tripod. On the way to Glacier Point the road ascends quite rapidly to a final altitude of over 2000 feet above the valley floor.

The first light of dawn was evident behind Merced Peak as I approached the Bridalveil Creek area. To my right was Pothole Meadows–an area of odd, round pools of water about 5 feet in diameter which form bowl-shaped depressions in these meadows during the wet months of the melting snow in the spring and early summer.

As I approached the Sentinel Dome parking area, the sunrise was quite spectacular. I decided to gather my equipment for the mile hike to the summit. A short scramble over the rocks took me to the top where a wind-twisted Jeffrey Pine has grown from cracks in the bare granite. At this point there is a 360 degree panoramic view of the entire park. There is tremendous solitude atop Sentinel Dome. At sunrise it is as though the entire Sierra region is being created before your very eyes.

In dawn's light the exposure scale was somewhat short, but the shadows were long and well defined, as I set up my camera with a 7 1/4-inch Schneider Symmar S lens. To clear the early morning haze, and darken the sky and shadows, I used a No. 25 red filter. The deepest shadows of the tree were placed on Zone III. The clouds and the rock in sun fell between Zones VI/VII. I indicated Normal-plus-one development for the Super XX (ASA 200) film in D-25 for 21 minutes, followed by 3 minutes in a second bath of Kodalk without agitation.

The print is on Mitsubishi grade 3 developed in LPD (1:3) with 150cc Kodalk to one liter of stock. Toning is in selenium (1:20) for 8 minutes.

The early morning sun, casting long shadows across the surface of the dome, enhanced the qualities of this subject. For me, the effects of the early light are evident, relating in a very realistic fashion the aesthetic values of a subject such as this.

Grand Tetons and Jenny Lake
Grand Teton National Park, Wyoming

One beautiful storm-clearing afternoon I returned to the Grand Tetons from Yellowstone National Park. I had photographed in the Grand Tetons for four days before going to Yellowstone. The events of Yellowstone had not been that grand, due in part to all of the broken and detached matter from the previous summer fires. Earlier that morning there had been considerable rain storms in the area and the clouds were moving fast. With the clearing storm, the sky was filling with white, billowing thunderheads.

There is a road which winds along the banks of Jenny Lake. The view, quite spectacular in this remote area, displays the grand glaciers of South, Middle and Grand Teton (the tallest at 13,770 feet), and Mount Owen, Cascade Canyon, Hanging Canyon and Mount St. John.

Jenny Lake was gouged out by the mountain glaciers and is surrounded by substantial forests and vegetation. This habitat supports diverse wildlife. Grand Teton is one of my favorite places that I have had the privilege to photograph. The others are Yosemite National Park—and the Sierra Range which includes the Owens Valley—and the back country of Colorado.

There was a slight wind blowing across Jenny Lake as I set up my tripod with the 4 x 5 field camera. Using a 7 1/4-inch Schneider Symmar S lens, I composed the subject on the ground glass. I took numerous readings of various areas of the scene with my Pentax spot meter. The darkest part of the mountain forest was placed between Zones III/IV. The bright reflections of the lake fell between Zones V/VI; the clearing sky on VI and the bright clouds on VIII. The indicated exposure for Super XX film (ASA 100) was f 32 at 1/15 second. To clear the slight haze and assure some detail in the bright snow and clouds, I used a No. 8 yellow filter. Because of the filter, the adjusted exposure was f/32 at 1/8 second. The negative was developed normally in ABC Pyro for 10 minutes. The negative is printed on Mitsubishi grade 3 and is developed for 2 minutes in Glycin 130 (1:1), followed by toning in selenium (1:20) for 6 minutes. About 50 percent more exposure is given to the sky and clouds using a card with a hole in it, moving in a circular motion. There is a very subtle difference in too little or too much basic exposure with this image. With some earlier test prints, slightly more exposure was given and the fir forest on the mountain slope dried with too much density, depleting the highlights of the lake of sparkle. Less exposure in the print-making process resulted in a flatness unbecoming to the depth of the subject.

Reflections of Mount Moran
Grand Teton National Park, Wyoming

Towering to a height of more than 13,700 feet, the Grand Teton rises majestically above Jackson Hole. The Teton Peaks, of which there are seven that reach above 12,000 feet, are the youngest of the mountains in the Rocky Mountain system.

Within the range is Mount Moran, a chiseled-off flat peak that rises to 12,605 feet above the valley floor. A dozen glaciated canyons are visible within the region.

On this particular morning I was up before five and already in the park at sunrise. After photographing above the Snake River, I drove the road north, heading toward Jackson Lake. Aspen groves lined the road on both sides. As I approached a curve in the road, a mystical sight of unbelievable beauty lay spread out before me. Mount Moran in all its rugged splendor, lighted by early morning sun, was reflected in the calmness of a pond of near mirror quality. As I visualized the image before me, I immediately saw the final print in my mind's eye. I stopped along the road at several different points looking for the optimal reflection, before deciding on the place to set up my tripod and 4 x 5 field camera.

The first lens of a 7 1/4-inch focal length was too short. Changing to a 9 1/2-inch Nikkor gave me the exact field of view I had determined from my viewing card. To clear the morning haze and darken the blue sky, I used a No. 8 yellow filter. I spent considerable time taking numerous meter readings of the values within the subject. The pines at the left were placed on Zone III. The dark base of Mount Moran, the clear water in the pond and the foreground brush all fell on Zone IV. The sky fell on Zone V and the snows highlight fell on Zone VI, some-what lower than I wanted, even though the subject was quite somber. The exposure was made on Super XX (ASA 100) at f 45 at 1/8 second. To raise the highlights one Zone, or one stop, I developed the negative Normal-plus-one in Pyro. The print is on Mitsubishi grade 3 developed 30 seconds in Selectol Soft (1:1) followed by 2 minutes in Dektol (1:2). Toning in selenium (1:20) for 6 minutes adds considerable strength to the overall image.

Like Yosemite and Canyon de Chelly, I am in awe of nature's grand display of Grand Teton National Park–certainly to be in a class of the world's most beautiful natural treasures.

Cloud Reflections in Stream
Grand Teton National Park

It was a beautiful clear spring morning when I drove north through Grand Teton National Park. The air was fresh and the sun bright. Large billowing thunderheads filled the sky overhead.

I took an unmarked turn west near the far end of the park. The road, paved for the first few miles, winds up and down through meadows filled with blooming wildflowers. The road becomes gravel, narrowing and diverting in and out of lodgepole pine forest, and winds along the Snake River. There are numerous streams and ponds along the road, all tributaries to the Snake River. I walked along the banks of the streams, looking at reflections of clouds from different angles. At some angles they were very bright and clear, at others, obscured due to ripples in the water from a slight breeze. There also were bugs of various variety, darting in and out of the water, creating still further interruptions.

I went back to the car to get my tripod and camera case. I had brought my 4 x 5 Wista field camera and an assortment of six lenses, all of different focal lengths, and a dozen or more filters. My film at the time was Super XX, one of the few remaining thick emulsion films. The thick emulsion allows long development times, expanding the scale from pure black to pure white, applicable to the Zone System of photography developed by Ansel Adams and Fred Archer more than fifty years ago.

Setting up the camera was difficult, from the vantage point I wanted, due to the steep incline along the edge of the stream. I adjusted the tripod legs to various lengths, wedging them into rocks and mounds of dirt. My footing was extremely awkward to say the least. I finally was able to get in a position where I could compose the image on the ground glass. To maintain sharp focus from top to bottom, I used a slight tilt of the rear standard. With a spot meter, I took readings of all of the essential areas of the subject. Beginning at the low end of the scale, I placed the dark pine reflections on Zone III–the darkest part of the water also was on Zone III. The bright cloud reflections were placed on Zone VII. To raise the clouds, brightening them further, I indicated Normal-plus-1/2 development in ABC Pyro. With a No. 8 yellow filter in place I waited several minutes for the breeze across the stream to calm down, and then made the exposure on Super XX (ASA 100) at f 22/32 for 1/8 second.

The print is on Oriental Seagull grade 3 developed in Glycin 130 (1:1) for 3 minutes. For each liter of stock, I added 25cc of benzotriazole and 75cc of Kodalk–made from 20 grams to a liter of water. Toning is in selenium (1:20) for 4 minutes.

I have always been satisfied with this image as being of somewhat out of the ordinary aesthetics. A number of people have inverted it stating, "It almost works this way." I have no response to this attitude. Seldom do we stand on our head to view a situation of this type when we come across it.

It is an image of this composition that a photographer must check closely when it comes to reproduction in books or magazines; that the printer inadvertently does not get it turned upside-down during the stripping process.

Grand Tetons and the Snake River
Grand Teton National Park, Wyoming

The winter snows still dominate Grand Teton Peak in spring, as bright aspen foliage announces the beginning of a new season.

Upon seeing this magnificent range, I can fully understand just how it got its name. These grand, glacier covered peaks tower more than 13,000 feet above the majestic landscape that includes eight large lakes, many smaller ones, and forests rich with aspen, fir, pine and spruce.

The Snake River, originating at the southern end of Yellowstone, winds its way to Jackson Lake, exits the dam and flows the 27 miles within Grand Teton National Park.

I hiked and climbed many areas adjacent to the Snake, photographing along its forks and tributaries for several days early one June. The weather, warm and atmospherically clear most of the time, still had a limited amount of haze in late afternoon.

The image here was made about five o'clock one afternoon near the cross bridge at Moose Junction. The effects of the scene, and the light on the subject, were very vibrant. There was considerable haze between the aspen and the mountain range, typical of back-lighted subjects. To help separate the aspen on the right from the background, and add to the contrast of the mountain and snow, I chose a No. 11 light yellow/green filter. My camera was a 4 x 5 field camera with a 7 1/4-inch Schneider Symmar S lens. With a spot meter, I took extensive readings of all areas of the scene. The only deep black, the shaded side of the bridge, was placed on Zone II. The lower mountain in shade fell between Zones III/IV, and the aspen on the right on Zone V. The water fell on Zone VI, the snow on Zone VII and the clouds on Zone VIII. The basic exposure was 1/30 second at f 16. My adjusted exposure, due to the filter factor, was two stops more at 1/30 second at f 8. Normal development in ABC Pyro was indicated for the Super XX film (ASA 100).

The light green filter cleared the haze considerably and added more contrast, which enhanced the foreground/background separation. Early prints were made on various papers–Oriental Seagull, Mitsubishi and Galerie–but were not to my expectations. My decision to intensify the negative in selenium (1:1) for 10 minutes proved satisfying. The negative was submerged in the selenium, down only to the top of the water line. The water was never intensified. An increase of between 1/2 and 1 paper grade was achieved in the top 2/3 of the image, allowing the negative to print well on Mitsubishi grade 3 in Selectol Soft (1:1) for 45 seconds, followed by 1 3/4 minutes in Dektol (1:2) with 25cc benzotriazole per liter of stock developer. The low values are further intensified by selenium toning (1:20) for 8 minutes. A higher paper grade would have achieved many of the desired values, however, subtle gray tones in the rushing water would have been lost making the water harsh in appearance.

The Grand Tetons, Ranch and Thunderheads
Grand Teton National Park

This was the last image made during the last day in the Grand Tetons, on a trip that included Colorado, New Mexico and Arizona.

For five days I had photographed this grand and glorious national park. From the Snake River to the backcountry—from the meadows to the mountain peaks—the beauty was everywhere.

This particular morning I had spent hours in numerous aspen groves with my 4 x 5 field camera. The day was especially bright and the sun warm and energizing. Not a tree branch was stirring along Slide Lake on the eastern boundary of the park.

I had packed up all of my equipment, and was returning to the center of the park by way of an old gravel road, when I came upon a cattle ranch set in a meadow of millions of blooming dandelions enveloped by the wonder of the Teton Range. Thunderheads were everywhere, and possible photographs were on my mind as I stopped the car near the cattle crossing. I set up my wooden tripod and field camera along the side of the road. I did not keep a record of the lens used, but considering the size of the thunderheads, I am sure it was of either a 3 1/2-inch or 7 1/4-inch focal length. I do know that I used a No. 25 red filter and a polarizer to darken the blue sky, giving the clouds fullness and dimension. I took various readings with a spot meter, placing the dark of the mountains on Zone IV (lowered by the two filters)— the bright clouds fell on VII. I waited a considerable length of time for the clouds, sun and shadows to all move in the right position. The clouds at high altitude would form perfectly only to break apart seconds later.

I wanted well contained edges that were free of straggling remnants. I noticed too, that at times the lower part of the mountains would become shaded, adding good contrast and separation from the range behind. I waited for a combination of good cloud structure, and sun and shade moving across the foothills, and then at just the exact second, made the 1/8 second exposure at f 11/16 on Super XX (ASA 100). The negative was developed Normal-plus 1/2 in ABC Pyro.

This negative prints well on Mitsubishi grade 2 paper with split development in Selectol Soft (1:2) for one minute followed by Dektol (1:2) for two minutes. It is then toned in selenium (1:20) for 6 minutes. I turned the holder over to make a duplicate exposure, but in a few seconds the clouds had moved and began breaking apart, and the shade on the low mountains in front had cleared away.

This photograph is a good representation of the visualized image in my mind's eye, with strong cloud formations against a black sky.

Aspens, Morning Sun
Grand Teton National Park

On my last day photographing in Grand Teton National Park I was up before sunrise and down by the Snake River, hiking along one of the many trails. The Snake, which runs 27 miles within the park, glittering in the early morning light, swells each spring with winter meltwater.

This particular morning was spent looking for aspen groves I had not visited before on this trip. On the main road there is a turn off at Gros Ventre Junction which winds through pastures, meadows, dozens of aspen groves, and past Slide Lake to Atherton Creek, Red Hills and Crystal Creek. I have always been fascinated by the aspen, a beautiful tree of the poplar family, that thrives at the higher altitudes of Wyoming, Colorado and New Mexico. The aspen is graceful, strong and sturdy, yet transparent in a photogenic way any season of the year. I was now literally among thousands of aspens. The sun shone westward across their bright surface, adding beautiful natural contrast to the forest. I looked for the perfect composition. There were so many trees the choice was endless.

I made numerous exposures in the area. Some were of single trees, some of just a few selected ones, and others of entire groves. At one point I looked up and immediately saw the final image against the blue sky. I tilted the 4 x 5 camera upward toward the tree tops and sky, but could not include enough of the lower tree trunks using the 7 1/4-inch lens, so I changed to a 3 1/2-inch Schneider Angulon. The composition was just right and the shorter lens gave me considerably more depth of field, allowing sharp focus from the lowest trunk to the tree tops. This is a case where an extreme convergence of the trees, and a forced perspective, works to the advantage of the subject.

The spot meter informed me of a four-stop scale from dark to light. The darkest part of the trees fell between Zones III/IV. The early morning sun fell between Zones VII/VIII. The sky was low, on Zone IV, where I wanted it. To lighten the leaves against the sky, I used a No. 8 yellow filter. The basic exposure was f 32 at 1/10 second but the filter factor added one stop to f 32 at 1/5 second. I gave the Super XX (ASA 100) negative normal development in ABC Pyro. The print, with edge and corner burn-ins, is representative of the visualization at the time of exposure. I use Mitsubishi grade 3 paper developed in Edwal Ultra Black (1:7) for 2 minutes followed by toning in selenium (1:20) for 8 minutes.

Aspens and the Grand Tetons, Slide Lake Road
Grand Teton National Park, Wyoming

In all of the trips I have taken to the High Country, the aspen has to be at the top of the list when it comes to exciting photographic subjects. I have always found pleasing compositions of wonderful contrasts in their blacks, grays and whites.

Visualization, and seeing the final print in my mind is very exciting. Once the composition is achieved, the photograph must be made from that precise position. Moving the camera as much as an inch or two in any direction will surely create tangents, mis-alignments or unpleasing compositions. Changing to lenses of different focal lengths is the only acceptable change which can be made. A change of *focal length* will bring a subject closer, or move it further away, while retaining exactly the same perspective. Moving the *camera* closer or further back from the subject is entirely different, and will change the entire composition. This can certainly be proven when photographing a subject between posts or through a number of trees.

If the right focal length lens *is not* available, once the image has been composed correctly using a card with a 4 x 5 cut-out, the next shortest focal length should be used. We can then crop this somewhat larger image when a print is being projected in the enlarger.

This photograph was made on a clear and very warm spring morning along the Ventre road in the Slide Lake area of the Grand Tetons. I arrived just after sunrise and waited a considerable length of time for the light to shine across the tree trunks. The luminous scale was long, about seven Zones (or stops). To retain the feeling of the shade within the grove, and to clear the distant haze in front of the mountain range, I used a No. 8 yellow filter on a 7 1/4-inch Schneider Symmar S lens on my 4 x 5 field camera of wood construction.

With my spot meter, I moved to within inches of the tree trunks to take accurate readings of the black knots, the darkest values of the entire subject. They were placed between Zones I/II. The shady side of the tree trunks fell on Zone IV, as did the tall grass which was in part shade and part sun. The blue sky fell between Zones VI/VII, and was reduced in value due to the yellow filter. The sun's highlights on the trees, and the snow on the mountains, fell on Zones VII and VIII respectfully. The negative was exposed for 1/2 second at f 45 on Super XX (ASA 100), and was developed in ABC Pyro.

The print is on Mitsubishi grade 2 developed in D-72 (1:2) with 20 grams of Kodalk per liter of stock, and 25cc benzotriazole per liter of stock. The print is toned in selenium (1:20) for 6 minutes.

Aspen Detail
Grand Teton National Park

Twenty-five years ago I was painting landscapes as well as photographing them. I would photograph the landscapes on color negative film and make type C prints for reference, and then paint watercolors from them. The Art of Photography was the means-to-an-end—The Painted Art.

Nearly sixty years ago in San Francisco, painters protested the use of gallery space for the exhibition of photography. Their claim—photography was not an art form. It was Ansel Adams and his newly formed f/64 Group that fought those protests and pursued the establishment of photography in museums and art galleries. Although photography is well received and IS considered an art form, to this day there are some areas of the country where black-and-white photography is not understood.

Having both painted and photographed the landscape, I am thoroughly convinced that photography is every bit as much creative art. In fact, I find that with absolute knowledge of the craft, both visual and technical, one can interpret, respond and create the natural scene on film and paper in dramatic ways that no other medium can.

Although Aspen Detail shown here is rather abstract in feeling—or stylized, as is more preferred—it is very true to the actual subject as it appeared. To accent detail and textures, I looked at many tree trunks within a grove between Grand Teton National Park and Yellowstone. To obtain the effect I wanted, I had to find the right tree in the correct position to the sun in order to enhance the curvature, and have skimming shadows across the sur-

face. The trees in the area were quite large–this one was about 18-inches in diameter. The section I preferred was almost at eye-level, and required a high position for my 4 x 5 view camera.

From several feet back the tree trunk looked to be of average to high contrast, however, in taking readings with my spot meter, I found the scale to be rather short– probably because of the highlights being light greenish/ gray and not pure white. The black knots were placed between Zones II/III. The shady side of the trunk fell on Zone III and the brightest part in sun only as high as Zone V (middle gray). The Super XX (ASA 200) film was exposed with a 7 1/4-inch Schneider Symmar S lens at f 45 for 1/8 second, and developed Normal-plus-one in ABC Pyro. I was not sure that raising the high values from Zone V to VI would be sufficient, but did not want to lose detail and texture at the high end of the scale. The negative prints well on Mitsubishi grade 2 paper developed for 2 minutes in D-72 (1:2) with 25cc of benzotriazole added per liter of stock, and 10 grams of Kodalk per liter of stock, followed by selenium toning for 6 minutes.

Surging Waters, Tower Creek
Yellowstone National Park

The spectacular canyons of the Yellowstone River provide a glimpse of earth's interior as waterfalls highlight the boundaries of lava flows and thermal areas. Yellowstone National Park, the Grand Old Park, was the world's first national park (1872), and is also one of the largest. The central portion of the park is essentially a broad, elevated volcanic plateau.

I had arrived early one chilly spring morning to photograph in the park's southern end. There was a light drizzle which turned to rain by mid-morning. Not wanting to get all of my view camera equipment wet, I chose to shoot 35mm color transparencies of accessible areas. I did not spend long periods of time out and about as the rain was quite hard at times. Much of the area, too, was quite disappointing due to the remnants of the fires of the previous summer.

The photograph shown here was made at Tower Creek at the base of the 120-foot Tower Fall. The rain had subsided by early afternoon as I set up my 4 x 5 field camera in the rocky crevices by the swirling rapids of the creek. The legs of the tripod were wedged between the rocks at the extreme edges. I placed my camera case with film, filters and various lenses between two large boulders which shielded the equipment from the spray and mist of the turbulent rushing water. Because of the position of the tripod and camera, it was very difficult composing the image. I had to twist, turn and stretch in an awkward position to see the image on the ground glass. My spot meter gave sporadic readings, fluctuating 3 to 4 stops due to the surging water. As near as I could determine, the low values of the rocks were placed on Zone III. The water in shade fell on Zone V, and the water highlights in sun fell on Zone VIII. To strengthen the shadows within the water, I used a No. 8 yellow filter on my 7 1/4-inch Schneider Symmar S lens. The exposure for Surging Water, Tower Creek, was made on Super XX (ASA 100) for 1/15 second at f 11. I made quite a number of negatives of different compositions of this subject at various shutter speeds.

The negative was developed normally in ABC Pyro. First prints were on Mitsubishi grade 3 developed for 2 minutes in Bromophen (1:3). I find better resolution and added strength to the subtleties in the water by developing the print in Selectol Soft (1:1) for 1 minute, followed by 2 minutes in Dektol (1:2). LPD (1:3) for 2 minutes is also an excellent choice following the Selectol Soft. Toning is in selenium (1:20) for 5 minutes.

Aspens
McClure Pass, Colorado

I arose very early one spring morning in Glenwood Springs, Colorado and headed south through the Elk Mountains and toward Ouray. I had planned to take as many back roads as I could on this trip. The altitude in Glenwood Springs is 10,850 feet. By the time I had reached the McClure Pass I was at 8700 feet.

As I was driving along, I came to a stand of aspens of serene quality. The early morning sun was just beginning to skim the surfaces of the large tree trunks. I parked the car along the edge of the road and carried my equipment to the scene. The subject was very still and the light soft and impressive. I was using my 4 x 5 field camera on a sturdy wooden tripod. I looked at the image on the ground glass as I composed the subject. The grove was full of aspens and I was having difficulty composing and getting correct and accurate perspective in the camera. The tree spacing and alignment was not working to my satisfaction. Taking a framing card from my camera case, I began to view the subject through the 4 x 5 window, composing, as I walked closer, then further back–then to the right and to the left. Finally I found the spot which allowed for true alignment leaving the appropriate spacing between the tree trunks. Moving just a few inches in any direction, forward or backward, changed the entire composition. Marking the exact spot with a rock, I moved the tripod with camera to the new position. This shows the important use of a framing card to compose and isolate the subject, and give clean edges, eliminating unwanted surrounding elements of a scene.

The sun was becoming more intense, showing a roundness to the tree trunks, as I began taking readings with my spot meter. I placed the dark forest background between Zones II/III. The green foliage fell on Zone IV and the shaded side of the trees on Zone V. The highlighted sides fell on Zone VII. To assure brightness to the tree trunks, I developed the Super XX (ASA 100) negative Normal plus 1 in ABC Pyro. The lens was a 7 1/4-inch Schneider Symmar S at f 32 for 1/2 second. No filter was used.

The print is on Mitsubishi grade 3 developed in Edwal Ultra Black 1:7 (with 25cc of 10% Potassium Bromide per liter of stock developer) for 2 minutes, and toned 7 minutes in selenium (1:20). About 100 percent more exposure is given using a card to burn-in both sides, from the print edges to the two outer tree trunks. Top, bottom and corner edges receive an additional 40 percent burn.

My decision to take the back roads around Crested Butte and Gunnison, about 60 miles through the Kibler Pass, was a particularly good one. The drive through the pass had to be about the most beautiful country I have ever seen. There were gigantic mountains of great splendor with millions of aspens in groves everywhere. Rivers, lakes and deep canyons were filled with fresh, bright green corn lilies. The 60 degree temperature felt wonderful. The usual afternoon thunderstorms with hard rain came up and hampered my photography, but they cleared early and considerable time was still left. I made about a dozen exposures of an array of waiting subjects. Every day should end so grand!

Fir Forest
McClure Pass, Colorado

There is a mystique about Colorado. It is hard to put into words the glorious feelings I get when traveling and photographing in this high country. Hopefully, my feelings and emotions are reflected in the photographs I make. There are purple mountains with green meadows as far as the eye can see. The subjects are very inspirational.

After photographing aspen groves in the early morning light in McClure Pass, I proceeded southward to Ouray. The landscape along the way was beautiful and the mountains rich with spring wildflowers.

In McClure Pass it was warm, calm and peaceful, in total contrast to the experience at the high altitudes in Rocky Mountain National Park a few days before. There I ran into severe winter weather where the temperature dropped from 60 to 30 degrees in about twenty minutes. I encountered rain, sleet and snow with clouds down to the highway. The inclement weather, quite worrisome at times, made for generally a bad day, somewhat surprising as the forecast was for good, warm sunny weather. The weather, no matter how spectacular to the eye, can be of major concern when it comes to working with a large view camera. I finally had to give up at the 14,000-foot altitude and move considerably lower.

The hundreds of aspen groves are breathtaking in McClure Pass. Capitol Peak, at 14,130 feet, overshadows other majestic mountains in the Elks Range.

As I was driving along, I came upon a tall and powerful mountain, covered with fir trees. What caught my eye was the symmetrical composition. The trees were lined up horizontally and vertically in perfect order. I stopped

the car and set up my 4 x 5 view camera with a 12-inch lens (300mm). Although the scene was of low contrast, I visualized the final print as being strong with higher luminous values. At the distance I was from the subject, I was only able to take a reading of the dark fir trees within the composition. That value was places between Zones II/III. The Sun's highlight on the tips of the trees was too small to get an accurate reading, therefore, calling on experience, I judged the higher values to be about 1 to 1 1/2 Zones higher, or about Zone III/IV. I indicated Normal-plus-2 development in ABC Pyro for the Super XX (ASA 100) film exposed at f 8/11 for 1/60 second. This moved the high values (placed between Zones III/IV) to Zone V. Given the conditions, I could not see where a filter would have accomplished anything better.

First prints, made on Galerie grade 4, were not as intense as I had hoped for at the time of exposure. Since then, the negative has been intensified in selenium (1:2) for 10 minutes, with continuous agitation, expanding the contrast about one additional Zone to around VI, much more to my original visualization.

Recent prints, with much more solidity after intensification, are on Mitsubishi grade 4 developed in Dektol (1:2) for 2 minutes with 25cc benzotriazole per liter of stock, and selenium toned (1:20) for 6 minutes.

Sagging Gate
Leadville, Colorado

A trip through Colorado can encourage anyone to click away the shutter of a camera. The beauty is endless in the Rocky Mountains, especially in spring and fall.

On this particular trip I had taken many of the old dirt roads through the backcountry looking for new subjects to photograph.

I was driving south from Breckenridge one early morning in June, when I came to Leadville, a unique gold and silver mining town of the 1800's. Leadville lies at an altitude that makes its climate rigorous even by Rocky Mountain standards. Hundreds of houses and buildings still stand from the gold mining days when there were more than 30,000 residents.

I still enjoy walking its gravel streets through neighborhoods of the old days. There are literally thousands of photographic possibilities in Leadville. Its heritage has been preserved in tact from the Healy House of 1878 to the Dexter cabin—home of James Dexter, one of the states early millionaires.

I was exploring the town quite early in the morning, tripod in one hand and camera case in the other. Considering the altitude of over 10,000 feet, the air was pleasant and the temperature mild. I photographed an old express depot, a laundry truck— the phone number "71" told me it was of '40s vintage— and several other buildings, all more than a hundred years old. While walking through the alleys, I came upon an old weather-beaten garage with a dilapidated fence and sagging gate. I immediately saw the final photograph in my mind's eye. I set up my 4 x 5 field

camera with a 7 1/4-inch Schneider Symmar S lens. While I was composing the image, I realized that the weeds, foliage and dandelions at the base would blend into the wood of the gate. Therefore, I decided to use a No. 8 yellow filter for better separation. With my spot meter, I took readings, placing the dark background wall of the garage between Zones II/III–the gate fell on Zone III, not a great deal of separation between the two. The green leaves of the foliage fell between V/VI and the blooms of the dandelions VI/VII. In addition to the yellow filter, to help separate values, I indicated Normal-plus-one development in ABC Pyro. To hold as much depth of field as possible, the lens was set at f 22. The alley acted as a tunnel and because of severe wind conditions, and clouds covering the sun, I had to wait more than twenty minutes to make the final exposure on Super XX (ASA 100). Finally, there was a lull in the wind and I tripped the shutter for the 1/4 second exposure.

Printing the negative is a little complex. Mitsubishi grade 2 was too soft and grade 3 gave too much harshness to the wood grain. I finally settled on Mitsubishi grade 3 developed in Selectol Soft (1:1) for 1 1/2 minutes followed by LPD (1:4) for 1 1/4 minutes, and then toning in selenium (1:20) for 10 minutes. To help separate the wall of the garage from the gate, I burn in the background 50 percent more using a card with up and down passes to the top of the gate. With a hole in a card I burn in the dandelion blooms 100 percent of the basic exposure.

Poplar Trees in Afternoon Light
Sawpit, Colorado

After photographing in Ouray, Colorado one morning, I decided to drive north along the San Juan mountains. I passed through Ridgeway on my way to Telluride. Along the way I passed numerous tree groves of pines and aspens nestled against mountain cliffs of bright gray granite. The air was calm and warm. The light very clear and bright.

Ouray and Telluride are separated by the Uncompahgre Mountain Range. It stood to reason that in 1875 all the silver and gold veins in Ouray would also show through on the westside. This was the case on the gray granite mountainside above the headwaters of the San Miguel River. Telluride flourished rapidly and it developed a reputation of wide repute. The town felt the effects of Butch Cassidy when he withdrew more than $25,000, without authorization. The town is surrounded by high walls of granite with 300 foot waterfalls.

I was driving through Sawpit when I came upon a grove of beautiful poplars in the afternoon light. With the highlights glistening in the bright sun, I set up my 4 x 5 field camera at the edge of the grove. Using a spot meter, I took readings of the dark tree trunks, ground shadows and the bright highlights in sun. To eliminate the background skylight showing through the tree tops, I used a 9 1/2-inch Nikkor lens. Using Super XX (ASA 100), I placed the low values on Zone III with the highlights falling between Zones VI/VII. The No. 11 light green filter raised the highlights somewhat, along with Normal-plus-one development in ABC Pyro for 12 minutes.

I had intended for slightly higher values, but inadvertently figured the adjusted exposure for the green filter at a one stop increase (1/15 at f 16 to 1/8 at f 16) when it should have been plus two stops. The negative is very good, however, with a good range of values.

The image is printed on Arista Classic grade 2 developed in Glycin 130 developer (1:1) for 3 minutes, followed by toning in selenium (1:20) for 7 minutes to intensify the values. The print is a very real interpretation of the scene as it actually appeared at the time I made the photograph. I find it quite serene and full of warmth and brightness.

I made several other photographs in the area that afternoon, but this image was the most expressive of the region.

Cascade Fall: A Fantasy
Ouray, Colorado

I arrived back in Ouray in early afternoon after photographing groves of lodgepole pines near Sawpit. The sun was warm and the air crisp and clear.

I drove to the top of 8th avenue and parked the car. I assembled my camera equipment, tripod and film holders and began the hike up to Cascade Fall. The trail is fairly steep and requires climbing over and around many rocks and boulders of considerable size. The humidity was extremely low (9 percent), and the air very dry. Caution was necessary when hiking at the high altitude above Ouray–7700 feet. Dehydration is a common factor and without sufficient liquid it is impossible to climb steep inclines. I stopped to rest several times during the hour climb, which ends right at the base of the fall.

The scene was quite spectacular. Even though the spray from the fall was heavy, I moved as close as I could get. I set up my camera, wedging the tripod legs in between the rocks. I had to keep the camera covered with my focusing cloth as the spray was soaking at times. I was so close to the base of the fall that I had to tilt the camera at almost a 90 degree angle, straight up to the top. I first tried a 9 1/2-inch lens, but it did not bring the subject close enough, so I changed to a longer focal length of 12-inches.

After making one exposure of the upper fall, I lowered the camera and photographed the base. The subject then became almost a fantasy. To render good shadow detail in the water highlights, I used a No. 8 yellow filter. Using my spot meter, I placed the darkest part of the rocks on Zone II, the highlights of the water fell on Zone VIII. The indicated exposure was f 11 at 1/15 second.

With a one stop increase due to the filter factor, I gave an exposure of f 11 at 1/8 second. If I was to do this over, I would place the darkest parts of the rocks on Zone III and give N-1 development.

Usually I use a slower shutter speed when photographing water falls, but the water was dropping so rapidly, that I knew 1/8 second was slow enough to show sufficient movement and the softness I wanted. I used Super XX (ASA 100). Developing the negative in ABC Pyro retained all of the detail in the water highlights. To emphasis the silvery effect and brightness of the water, I burn-in, darkening the outer edges, corners and lower one quarter of the image 100 percent of the basic exposure.

The print, made on Mitsubishi grade 3 developed 30 seconds in Selectol Soft (1:2), followed by 2 minutes in LPD (1:3), is toned in selenium for 8 minutes.

Poppies and Stone Wall
Ouray, Colorado

After photographing beautiful thunderstorms at the high altitudes of Colorado, I was ready for a change of pace. I headed south and came to the beautiful town of Ouray (YouRAY) nestled along the San Juan Mountain range.

Ouray, which gets its name from the eminently wise Ute chieftain, was spawned by the mineral wealth extracted from the mines. In 1875, Ouray came alive with the first silver strike, which yielded more than $7 million over the next ten years. It was gold, however, that created great wealth and the Panic of 1893.

One beautiful crisp morning I arose before dawn, as usual, and set out to survey this quaint, old, but still very active mining town. I was carrying my case with a 4 x 5 field camera, six lenses, a light meter and an assortment of filters, six film holders with Super XX film and my wooden tripod. I was walking several blocks from the town, when I came upon a garden of orange poppies in full bloom. I set up my camera and composed the image on the ground glass. There was considerable wind blowing—with gusts quite strong at times. Because of the wind I knew I would need to use as fast of shutter speed as possible.

The field of poppies were against a dark pine tree background. Because of the value of the orange being close to that of the pines, I knew I would need an orange filter to raise their value considerably, and to also lower the pines behind them. To keep the background of pines full, I used a 9 1/2-inch lens. The longer lens caused a shallower depth of field than I would have otherwise preferred. A reading with the spot meter told me the background pines fell on Zone III and the poppies on Zone VI. To expand the scale, I indicated Normal-plus-two development, which raised the value of the poppies to Zone VIII (a two-stop increase). To hold the depth of field, I set the lens at f 11/16 at 1/8 second. With a two stop increase for the No. 15 orange filter, the adjusted exposure was f 11/16 at 1/2 second—slower than I would have liked. I inserted a film holder with Super XX at an ASA of 100, and waited a long time for the wind to die down. The down draft caused quite a disturbance, first in one area, then another. When a calm finally came, I made the exposure. The image is sharp to about the back row of poppies, where there was a slight disturbance. If I had this to do over, I would move the camera back about two feet, giving me a greater depth of field, increasing sharpness, then cropping the image slightly all around. Using a shorter focal length of lens would have accomplished greater depth of field, but would have also included background sky and other unwanted clutter.

The Normal-plus-two negative was developed in ABC Pyro for 15 1/2 minutes. The image is printed on Mitsubishi grade 3, developed in Selectol Soft (1:1) for two minutes followed by 1 1/2 minutes in Edwal Ultra Black (1:11) and toned in selenium (1:20) for 8 minutes.

Threatening Thunderstorm
Granby, Colorado

I had been in and out of thunderstorms for two days, beginning with severe winter like weather in Rocky Mountain National Park, and continuing in Breckenridge and Dillon. Both approaching storms and clearing storms are ideal for making fine expressive photographs. The time, however, during a storm can curtail all endeavors with the camera. I have always found it fascinating how storms develop and form within the confines of mountainous regions, creating depth and beauty even at their most perilous moments.

I do understand the dangers of storms, and do not stand in open areas or at high places with a tripod and camera containing a number of metal parts which act as a conductive lightning rod.

The ominous cloud formations associated with a storm breaking up is almost always a beautiful sight to behold. Very dramatic effects can be obtained photographically with the use of a red or green filter, and at times, in combination with a polarizer.

The weather, no matter how spectacular to the eye, can present problems if rain or wet snow is to be contended with. In the time it takes to set up a view camera, compose and take readings, it is possible to get a good soaking of self and equipment.

One spring afternoon I was driving south toward Granby, Colorado, aware of an approaching storm which was sure to bring rain. The sky was getting darker by the minute as the heavy clouds ahead moved in my direction.

At the outskirts of town, I pulled off the road and quickly set up my 4 x 5 field camera with a 3 1/2-inch Schneider Angulon lens. I knew I would have to work fast to keep from getting drenched. With my spot meter, I took readings of the subject. The dark mountain was placed on Zone IV–the dark clouds also fell on Zone IV. The bright clouds, still quite brilliant, fell high on the scale at Zone IX. Using a No. 25 red filter to lower the shadows within the clouds, I made the exposure on Super XX (ASA 100). The basic exposure was f 45 at 1/5 second, however, because of a filter factor of 8X, my adjusted exposure was plus three stops at f 16 at 1/5 second. The negative, developed in ABC Pyro, is printed on Mitsubishi grade 3 developed in Dektol (1:2), and selenium toned for 10 minutes. The negative is somewhat on the soft side and requires considerable burn-in of dark areas of the clouds to give solidity.

As soon as I made the exposure and packed up heading for town, the storm broke loose with torrential rain that lasted a good half an hour.

Upper Fall, Wolf Creek Pass
Road to Del Norte, Colorado

I have had many exciting times photographing water-falls in the high countries of numerous national parks. Some of those were Vernal Fall, Bridalveil Fall, Nevada Fall and Yosemite Falls, all in Yosemite National Park. With subjects of this nature, and if one knows their craft well, it is not difficult making elegant and handsomely composed photographs of scenes of such monumental proportions. Gigantic waterfalls are so picturesque, almost anyone can come away with a pleasant representation of the subject. There is tremendous power and force behind these soaring, falling, thundering waters of nature—some more than one thousand feet high. Then there are those only several feet high, such as Fern Springs in Yosemite, that emulate their counterparts in a delicate sort of way.

About seven o'clock one morning I was driving east from Durango through Wolf Creek pass on the road to Del Norte, Colorado. The air was fresh and clear and the sun extremely bright. As I made the curve in the road, there before me was a beautiful waterfall, thundering over glistening granite rocks. I was in such a hurry to make a photograph of the subject, I almost ditched the car. The water was booming over the edge, falling furiously to a pool below. I set up my 4 x 5 view camera with a 9 1/2-inch Nikkor lens. Although the height of the fall was about twenty feet above the road, the camera still was at a fairly steep tilt. I had to keep the lens cap on, as I was close to the base, and received a fair amount of spray from the water. Using my spot meter, I took readings of the dark rocks which were placed between Zones II/III, and the bright highlights of the water fell on Zone VIII. The luminance range was 5 1/2 Zones (or stops), quite appropriate for the subject. With a No. 8 yellow filter to give extra detail in the water's shadows, I made the exposure on Super XX (ASA 100) at f 8/11. The water was moving extremely fast, so to show a reasonable amount of movement I used a shutter speed of 1/15 second. The negative was developed in ABC Pyro and the print made on Mitsubishi grade 2 in Edwal Ultra Black (1:7) with benzotrizolc for 2 1/2 minutes, followed by toning in selenium for 5 minutes.

I made another exposure using a 12-inch Commercial Astragon lens for a tighter view, but the negative using the 9 1/2-inch lens made for a better composition.

Lower Fall and Pool, Wolf Creek Pass
Road to Del Norte, Colorado

After making two previous exposures of the upper fall, I moved the tripod and camera to the opposite side of the pool. Although the exposure and technical aspects were the same, the emotional response was different in photographing the pool. The visualized image was quite different in composition. The upper fall had considerable sunlight on the highlights of the water. The water at the point of impact in the pool had not yet received sunlight, therefore, the negative is of slightly less contrast. To compensate for a difference in lighting, and as a balance between the two images, Lower Fall and Pool is printed on Mitsubishi grade 3.

Photographing a subject of this nature has always been emotionally rewarding. This is a case where visualization worked to the fullest extent by capturing the intensity of the subject, and through the controls of the negative and printing process, transfers the emotional response to the viewer.

Sunrise
Taos, New Mexico

The trip east across Southern Colorado and southward into New Mexico was a most spectacular event. The early morning air was always crisp and clear and generally free of rain storms. Occasionally there was evidence of thunderstorms at a distance, but I did not encounter such weather early in the day.

As the noon sun began to warm, gigantic, billowing thunderheads would form and by 3:00 or 4:00 o'clock severe downpours would begin, lasting a couple of hours, and then clear to spectacular skies once again.

One morning though, on my drive south of Taos, severe storm clouds were evident around sunrise. The sun's rays beamed their way through any small opening in the clouds, at times shining only on Taos itself. I pulled off the main road about 300 feet, and drove a dirt road which wound up and down through the rocks and desert scrub. Finding a hilly point which gave me a good view of the Taos terrain, I set up my tripod and 4 x 5 field camera. I wanted to show the wide expanse of the scene, so I chose a 7 1/4-inch Schneider Symmar S lens (a normal lens for the 4 x 5 format), rather than a long lens which would have cropped out a good portion of the clouds. The sun was rising fast and I knew I would have to visualize the image, take meter readings and make the exposure quickly before the sun's rays disappeared.

I placed the desert scrub in the foreground low on Zone II. The dark range of the Sangre de Cristo Mountains (Blood of Christ) fell on Zone IV—the dark gray clouds on Zone V and the light horizon just above the mountain range on Zone VI. Using Super XX (ASA 100),

I made the exposure at f 32 at 1/8 second. To raise the high values, I indicated Normal-plus-two in Pyro developer. A straight print from this negative is not as I visualized the image and it requires additional exposures to bring the values to the places originally perceived. The basic print exposure is 23 seconds. With a card, there is an additional 15 second burn-in of the clouds, from the mountain range up to the top. All sides and corners receive an additional burn-in of 6 seconds each. The print is on Mitsubishi grade 2 developed 2 1/2 minutes in Edwal Ultra Black (1:7), with a little benzotriazole added, and is toned 6 minutes in selenium.

Ladder and Adobe
Taos Pueblo, New Mexico

On this particular trip to Taos I was privileged to spend a day with the Taos Indians at the Taos Pueblo Reservation.

Located two miles north of Taos, there is 1000 years of tradition associated with this, the largest pueblo structure in the United States. Over the thousand years of continuous habitation, little has changed. Mud and straw adobe walls are still a way of life for the nearly 1700 Indians living there. The crystal clear waters of the Rio Pueblo de Taos, which originates high in the mountains, is still the main source for drinking, cooking and irrigation.

Photographing during my time at Taos Pueblo was a very rewarding experience. The Indians there are most cordial, many times showing me another area, or explaining their traditions and way of life. There is an uniqueness in the people. By our standards their living is hard, with no abundance of the every day necessities we take for granted. Many residents work outside of the reservations, however, much of their source of income is from beautiful handcrafted wares such as jewelry, moccasins and pottery.

The photograph shown here, Ladder and Adobe, was made in the afternoon. The sky was full of clouds when I set up my 4 x 5 field camera with a 7 1/4-inch Schneider Symmar S lens. I had to wait more than half an hour for a strong sunlight. Using my Pentax spot meter, I placed the dark shadows of the ladder and background wall on Zone III. The blue sky fell between Zones V/VI–the sun's highlight on the ladder fell on Zone VII. To darken the shadows further, and to lighten the orange adobe walls,

I used a No. 15 deep yellow filter for the f 22/32 1/4 second exposure on Super XX (ASA 100). Development was Normal-plus-1/2 in ABC Pyro. The print was made on Oriental Seagull grade 3 developed in Edwal Ultra Black (1:7) for 2 minutes, followed by toning in selenium (1:20) for 4 minutes.

Saint Francis Church
Ranchos de Taos, New Mexico

Saint Francis Church sits in the Ranchos de Taos Plaza, and is surrounded by Indian housing and dwellings. The culture of the area is Spanish, Indian and Anglo—all mingle yet remain distinct. Taos is three villages—Taos proper, Pueblo de Taos (San Geronimo de Taos) the main home of the conservative Indians, and Ranchos de Taos, the farming community.

Over the years I have seen a number of photographs of Saint Francis Church made by Ansel Adams, Paul Strand, Morley Baer and others, but did not realize the size and strength of this southwestern monument. This splendid Spanish church with its heavy buttressed structure measures 120 feet in length, and is one of the great architectural monuments.

I had decided earlier that I would try to photograph this beautiful church in an appropriate manner different from previous ones that I had seen. When I arrived, I was faced with limitations not previously envisioned. The exterior of the church was going through major renovations and scaffolding was dominant across the front facade.

Using a framing card (a black card with a 4 x 5 cut opening), I explored the grounds looking for compositions which eliminated views of construction workers. I was now forced to look for new angles that I had not seen before. As I walked on the near south side, a nice clean composition was evident. The sun was bright and the shadows very pronounced, with all angles parallel. I visualized the shadows deep black on the scale with two light areas in direct contrast. I set up my 4 x 5 field camera with a 9 1/4-inch Nikkor lens–a longer lens than a normal focal length of 7 1/4-inches. With readings from a spot meter, I placed the dark wall shadows on Zone III–the wall with the sun fell between Zones VI/VII. I used a No. 15 orange filter to darken the shadow areas and to lighten the bright orange facade. Further contrast of the Super XX negative was achieved with Normal-plus-one development in ABC Pyro. The print is on Mitsubishi grade 3 developed in LPD (1:3) for 2 minutes, followed by toning in selenium (1:20) for 8 minutes. A burn-in of 40 percent of the basic exposure is given to all sides, with 50 percent to the corners.

Cross and Sun, Saint Francis Church
Ranchos de Taos, New Mexico

I made a number of exposures at various positions while photographing this wonderful church of Spanish architecture.

After making the previous image, I turned the camera back toward the front tower and cross. Just as I had framed the tower I noticed the brightness of the sun's rays above the roof line. I stepped back and realized the sun was only a few minutes from rising over the edge. Using the same lens (a 9 1/4-inch) from the previous exposure, I inserted a film holder. With the reading from my spot meter, I placed the dark shaded tower on Zone III—the sunlight coming from the roof's edge was at least Zone VIII, and certainly was much higher as it rose up to the base of the cross—probably around Zone XV or higher. In order to eliminate blankness and assure detail in the basically silhouetted tower, I removed the No. 15 orange filter right before the exposure of 1/15 second at f 45. The Super XX (ASA 100) was developed normal in ABC Pyro. The print is on Galerie grade 3 developed in Edwal Ultra Black (1:7) and toned in selenium for 8 minutes.

Even though the scale was extremely long with very bright values high at the upper end, I was confident that the Pyro developer would hold the light flares around the cross.

This image has been a very satisfactory one for me as it accomplishes the technique of exposing extreme dark values to extreme high ones while maintaining subtle detail at both ends of the tone spectrum.

Drying Rack Shadow on Baking Horno
Taos Pueblo, New Mexico

The Indians of Taos Pueblo live in the largest structure of its kind in the country. Numbering 1700, they work at jobs off the reservation for the most part, but substantial income is derived from their producing hand-crafted pottery and jewelry, and from the baking and selling of bread.

Bread is baked in the traditional way in outdoor dome ovens just as the Indians have done for nearly 10 centuries. This dome oven is called a baking horno (pronounced orno). The Indian women still prepare the grain in the traditional way by winnowing it from a basket held high over their heads. This is a form of sifting the grain in the wind to free it from chaff, which are the husks of corn.

During the morning, I had made many photographs around the Pueblo. Some photographs were of the adobes and drying racks where meat is dried and cured. It was while I was visualizing an image at the far end of the pueblo that I turned and saw, in the high-noon sun, the image of the overhead drying rack shadow on a baking horno. I immediately turned my camera around and framed the subject on the ground glass. There were only two luminance values–one dark, the other light. The dark shadow was placed on Zone III and the sunlit part of the horno fell on Zone VI. To darken the shadow and lighten the brightest area, I used a No. 15 deep yellow filter. I made the exposure on Super XX (ASA 100) at f 16 for 1/15 second. To raise the high value, the negative was developed Normal-plus-two in ABC Pyro. Between the No. 15 filter and the two-zone expansion, I believe the scale to have been increased to about 4 1/2 Zones.

The print is on Mitsubishi grade 3 developed 2 minutes in Edwal Ultra Black (1:7) and toned in selenium for 6 minutes.

Although this is rather an abstract image, it is expressive of the Taos Pueblo Indians and their culture, and is a departure from the usual subjects associated with the reservation.

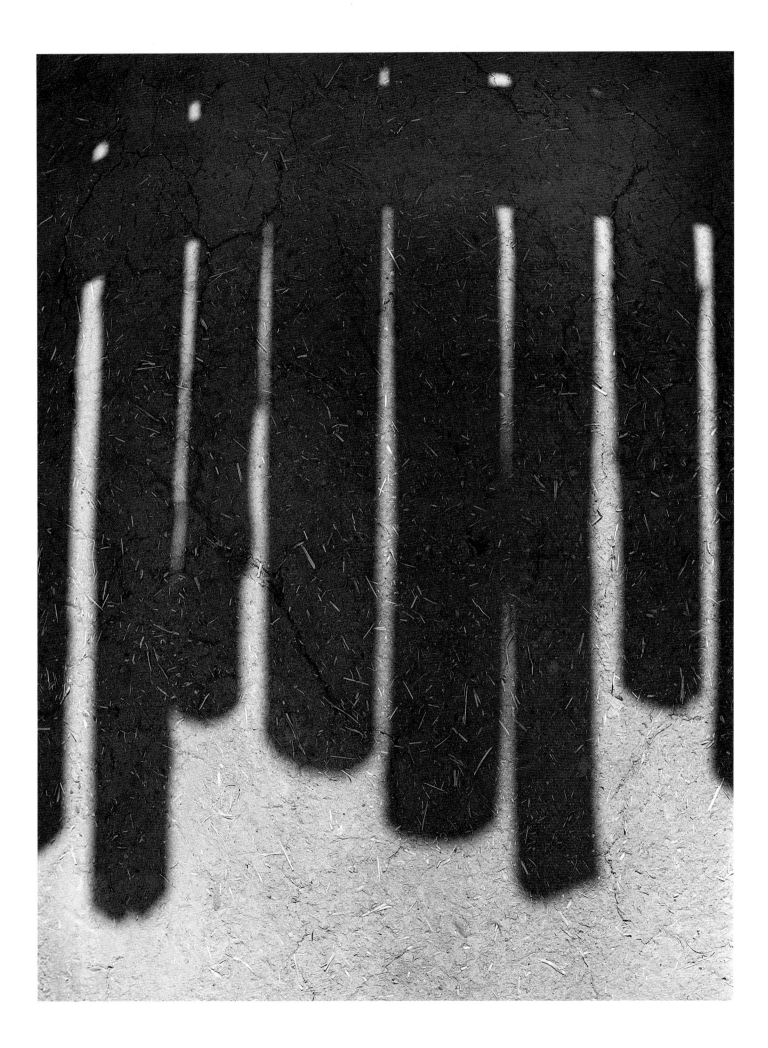

Adobes and Evening Storm
Taos Pueblo, New Mexico

Photographing in New Mexico has always brought extreme pleasure to me. I have a true appreciation for the land and the beauty associated with it, especially in the northern section around Espanola, Taos, the Chama Valley and at the Colorado border. As a photographer, my response to the land and the culture of New Mexico is quite different from the many other places I've been. So many images come to light, all new and different I am sure, from those captured on film by Paul Strand in years past.

There is a vastness, yet a closeness. The skies are clear, yet filled with billowing clouds. There is a chill in the air, yet the culture warms the heart. History has touched this great valley because of the Rio Grande, New Mexico's great river. For a thousand years the Indians have made this their domain. Gold and ore were never unearthed in the region. The Rio Grande, fed by the snows and springs of the San Juan Rockies, was always the most precious element of the earth. The sole source of water for Taos Pueblo is Red Willow Creek, originating at Blue Lake, high in the mountains between Taos Mountain and Mount Wheeler, the highest point—13,151 feet—in New Mexico.

I had my 4 x 5 view camera with me and was photographing near the South Pueblo when an afternoon thunderstorm began to approach. The sky was dark and ominous as I rapidly set up my camera in one of the deserted streets. While I was visualizing the image, the exposure values were shrinking rapidly. As the light was diminishing minute-by-minute, I could see the fine print developing in my mind. The light on the scene was extremely flat. I took quick readings with my spot meter, placing the dark door and under-side of the stoop between Zones II/III--the light walls and clouds fell on Zone VI. The facade was an orange/tan so I decided to try to lighten areas of the adobe the best I could by using a No. 15 deep yellow filter. The exposure was 1/30 second at f 8 on Super XX (ASA 100). The negative was developed Normal-plus-three in ABC Pyro. Early prints were on Mitsubishi grade 2 developed in Bromophen (1:3) for 2 minutes followed by selenium toning for 10 minutes. More recently I have used Oriental Seagull grade 3 or Arista Classic grade 3 in Glycin 130 (1:1) for 3 minutes.

The effect of this image has been quite pleasing, and is a good example of how visualization, control of exposure and development work together in producing the expressive fine art print.

Moonrise
Canyon de Chelly National Monument, Arizona

On a trip from New Mexico to Arizona I turned north at Gallop and headed for Canyon de Chelly in the Navajo Indian Reservation. The canyon houses many of the pueblo built apartment-style homes in caves or rock shelters above the floor. The Hopi Indians occupied the area after the 1300's, but today the Navajo use the canyon floor for farming and livestock grazing. The canyon is rich in beauty with its red sandstone walls which rise 1000 feet in a sheer, smooth ascent.

I spent the entire day photographing White House Ruins, Antelope House and Mummy Cave. I had numerous problems with the wind, so severe at times—estimated at nearly 60 mph—that it was all I could do to keep the camera and tripod from blowing over the cliff edge and descending to the rocks hundreds of feet below. I waited long periods at times to make exposures. The wind would gust, then die to complete calmness for a few seconds, only to blast even harder against the person and equipment. I had luck with a few exposures of the day, but a lot of negatives were ruined due to the lack of predicting wind velocity. I was not always accurate in determining its calm periods. I had thought of giving up several times but was ever-hopeful conditions would improve.

I had calculated the times of the moonrises for the month, and had determined this particular evening would be the correct one for photographing its rise near sunset. The location was a good one if the winds would cooperate and diminish.

Moonrises, and the photographing of them with both conventional cameras and lenses, and with telescopes, have always fascinated me. I selected an overlook where the direction was right. I set up my 4 x 5 field camera with a Schneider Symmar S lens of a focal length of 7 1/4-inches, and waited about one and a half hours. As the sun was getting low to the horizon behind me, the moon—about three days from full—was rising before me. I was hoping that by the time the moon was up to about 25/30 degrees, the sun would still be slightly above the horizon to light the tops of the cliffs across the gorge from me. I had estimated correctly. Taking several readings with my spot meter, I placed the dark of the canyon walls between Zones II/III–the sun on the top of the rim fell on Zone IV, the deep blue sky near Zone V. The moon fell correctly on Zone VII. The indicated exposure was f 8 at 1/30 second. I chose a No. 25 red filter to darken the sky and add contrast to the detail of the moon, thus adding three more stops for an exposure of f 8 at 1/4 second. To raise the value of the sun on the cliffs and the moon, I gave Normal-plus-2 1/2 in ABC Pyro developer. I have, since first prints, intensified the negative by giving it a submersion in selenium (1:3) for ten minutes with continuous agitation.

The print is on Mitsubishi grade 3 developed in D-72 (1:2) for 2 minutes. I added 10 grams of Kodalk and 25cc of 1% benzotriazole per liter of stock developer. Toning is in selenium (1:12) for 6 minutes. Considerable burning-in is done to the sky, adding 120 percent more exposure from the horizon up to the top of the image.

Spider Rock
Canyon de Chelly National Park, Arizona

Canyon de Chelly is in the Navajo Indian Reservation, which is situated in the northwest corner of Arizona. This region was habitat for four Indian tribes and their cultures, dating from AD 348 to 1300. The cliff dwellings and circular sunken structures were occupied by, first, the Basketmakers, then the Hopi Indians, Anasazis and today it is home of the Navajo.

Nature's architectural accomplishments are certainly evident in the grandeur of this beautiful sheer-walled canyon. The spectacular design of deep sculptured sandstone passages is amazing. The massive display of wind-blown sand which accumulated in layers hundreds of feet deep, is red in color and known as de Chelly (d-shay) sandstone. More of nature's masterpieces are seen below in the streams that wind through farms tilled by the Navajo. The physical nature of the Canyon de Chelly has always been very spiritual for the peoples who lived there.

This June day morning, I had been photographing around the top rim of the canyon from the White House Ruin trail, to Massacre Cave on the northern most end. About two hours before sunset, I drove around to the south rim to Spider Rock, a towering 800-foot sandstone spire. During the entire day of photographing, the wind had been extremely strong, estimated at 40 to 50 miles per hour. By late afternoon, the velocity had diminished considerably, allowing for a much steadier camera and tripod. I parked my car and walked the 1/4-mile trail to a cliff overlooking the canyon below. I set up my 4 x 5 field camera with a 7 1/4-inch Schneider Symmar S lens. The late afternoon sunlight had become soft, decreasing the quality of the shadows and contrast below. To lighten the highlights on the cliffs and Spider Rock, and to darken the shaded areas, I chose a No. 15 orange filter. Readings with my spot meter told me that the exposure scale of the scene was about 3 1/2-Zones (or stops). Knowing that the filter would reduce the shadows, I placed them between Zones III/IV. The sun on the floor of the canyon fell low between Zones IV/V. The sunny parts of the cliffs fell on Zone V, and the horizon on Zone VII. For the Super XX (ASA 100) film, I planned a two-zone expansion of the negative, and gave Normal-plus-two development in ABC Pyro. There is about a 25 percent burn-in of the sky at the top, and 20 percent to all sides of the image. The print is on Mitsubishi grade 3 paper, developed in Edwal Ultra Black (1:7) (with 25cc of 10% potassium bromide per liter of stock developer) for 2 minutes, and toned in selenium (1:20) for 7 minutes.

Window, Morning Sun
Mission San Xavier del Bac, Tucson, Arizona

I was up before dawn and headed for San Xavier del Bac Mission in Tucson. It was early spring and the morning had a chill in the air when I arrived at the mission. The White Dove of the desert, as it is called, shows brightly across the Tucson landscape. The structure stands freely on the Papago Indian Reservation and is a beautiful example of Spanish mission architecture. The domes, carvings, windows and flying buttresses distinguish it from other missions.

San Xavier del Bac Mission has been photographed many, many times over the years by numerous photographers. Its domes and arches have been captured on film in long expansive shots by visiting photographers. Although I have photographed the mission several times, I always enjoy the return visit to look for different views and angles.

On this early morning I spent about half and hour walking around the old structure. The sun was rising as I set up my tripod on the front portico. I could hear the first mass of the day beginning inside. I attached my 4 x 5 field camera to the tripod. I am not sure which lens I used, as I failed to include the information in my technical notes, however, I believe it was the 7 1/4-inch Schneider Symmar S, considering the distance to subject as I remember it. I composed the image on the ground glass as the sunlight began to brush across the surface of the front wall and window. The softness of the subject was very pleasing aesthetically.

Using my spot meter, I took various readings of the subject. The dark of the window was placed between

Zones II/III, the shade on the wall fell on Zone VI, the sun between Zones VI/VII. There was only 1/2 zone (or 1/2 stop) difference between the shade on the wall and the sun's highlights—two extremely close values. I used Super XX (ASA 100) film at f 32/45 for 1/8 second. Just as I was ready and pulled the slide for the exposure, the sun's light shone across the surface for about a minute, emphasizing the texture of the facade. In order to hold all of the subtle textures and details in the sun's light, I indicated Normal-plus-two development in ABC Pyro. All of the textures are enhanced on Galerie grade 3 developed in Selectol Soft (1:1) for 1 1/4 minutes followed by Dektol (1:2) for 2 minutes. The print is toned in selenium (1:20) for 6 minutes.

I have attempted to print this negative on many different papers over the last few years, but have not been able to attain the quality of light that I have with Galerie. This image loses considerable feeling when printed on a cold tone paper. The early morning sun across the surface becomes flat and lifeless.

Shadow of Iron Gate
Mission San Xavier del Bac, Tucson, Arizona

After photographing Window, Morning Sun at this old, and very aesthetically beautiful mission church, I roamed the grounds looking for other subjects. There was one area of the old wall and facade that I had been working with for some time, as well as trying to photograph a wall through an old iron gate. As I was picking up my tripod, preparing to move to another location, I turned and there on the ground before me I saw the shadow of an iron gate.

With my spot meter I began taking readings of the subject. The sunlight was still soft, and the intensity quite low. The scale was very short. The shadow was placed on Zone III–the sun on the ground fell on Zone V (only a two-stop luminance). The exposure was f 45 at 1/8 second on Super XX (ASA 100). To expand the scale considerably, I gave Normal-plus-two development in ABC Pyro. The contrast of the negative is very good and prints well on Mitsubishi grade 3 developed two minutes in Edwal Ultra Black (1:7), followed by toning in selenium for 7 minutes.

White Dove of the Desert
Mission San Xavier del Bac, Tucson, Arizona

Several years ago on one of my photographic trips to Tucson, I made the image, White Dove of the Desert, San Xavier del Bac. Although there had not been any severe thunderstorms or rain, the skies were filled with threatening clouds most of the afternoon. Sunset was approaching as I packed up my equipment and headed back to Tucson. As I was driving west, I noticed in the rear-view mirror, the brilliance of the mission facade against the dark mountain panorama. I stopped the car and walked about a hundred yards across a field, in front of the Indian cemetery. I set up my tripod and began framing the subject on the ground glass. I used a 4 x 5 Omega view camera with a 7 1/4-inch Schneider Symmar S lens. The sun was now very low on the horizon and shielded by numerous clouds. The subject was gray and the exposure scale short. I had to wait several minutes for a time when the clouds would open slightly, permitting the sun's rays to strike the white facade of the church. The exposure was 1/15 second at f 11 on Agfapan 100. Devel-

opment was Normal-plus-two in Rodinal (1:50) for 17 1/2 minutes. The basic exposure for the making of the print is 20 seconds on Mitsubishi grade 2. The clouds, from the hill up to the top, receive an additional 60 seconds. Using a card with a hole in it, in a circular motion, I give 36 seconds more exposure working back and forth across the top. The print, developed in Selectol Soft (1:1) for 1 minute, followed by 2 minutes in Edwal Ultra Black (1:7), is toned for 8 minutes in selenium (1:20).

The Boundary Cone
Oatman, Arizona

A trip through the Southwest can be fresh with unexpected photographic results. Although the land is dry and parched, its beauty is vast. One can find solace and greatness in these rugged mountains, guarded by dramatic skies filled with majestic clouds.

In July of 1980, I had taken a trip up through Utah and Bryce Canyon and Zion National Park. The grandeur of Arches National Park was overpowering with its design of rock formations held in nature's high esteem. By the time I had reached Kingman, Arizona, by way of Mexican Hat and Monument Valley, I had already exposed about sixty negatives–usually eight to ten in a day is considered a good number, and I was pleased, having been on the road only four days. From Kingman I drove the old winding road toward Oatman, a mining town of the gold rush era. The distance is not far, but the time is long due to the narrowness of the road with its sharp curves and bumpy surface. About half way through the pass I looked to the east. There, was a beautiful desert landscape spread across the plains. In the basin below was a grand mountain, a giant cone of ancient lava called the Boundary Cone, a name given to it in 1857 by Lt. Joseph Christmas Ives, a member of the Army Corps of Topographical Engineers. Ives recognized the fact that the 35th parallel passed through the middle of the cone, and he named it for the geographical line upon which the U.S. Government proposed to build a wagon road. Geologists suspect that a fortune in precious metals lies beneath the granite walls of the Boundary Cone.

I was using my 4 x 5 Omega view camera with a 7 1/4-inch Schneider Symmar S lens of extreme sharpness. I took several readings with a Pentax spot meter. Since there was no real large black areas that fell low on the exposure scale, the darkest gray areas were placed on Zone IV. I assumed any blacks too small to read with the meter would fall around Zone II. The brightest clouds fell between Zones V/VI. To assure my visualization of a black sky, I used a No. 25 red filter in combination with a polarizing filter. The exposure was f 8 at 1/30 second on Super XX (ASA 200), developed Normal-plus-two in D-25, followed by 3 minutes in Kodalk with no agitation. The negative, relatively thin but containing all of the tonal values and information of the scene, is printed on Mitsubishi grade 3 developed in Edwal Ultra Black (1:7) for 2 minutes, followed by toning in selenium (1:20) for 8 minutes.

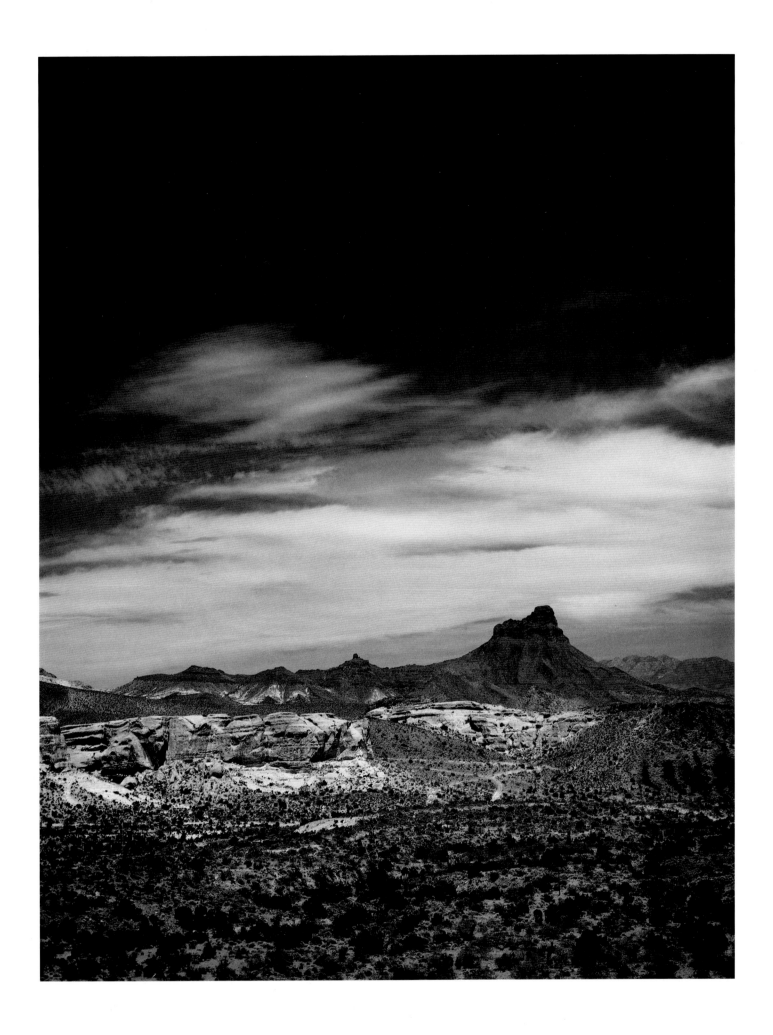

Calla Lily and Caladium
Lakewood, California

Visualization is the key factor to successful black-and-white fine art photography. With visualization we can interpret the values within the subject scene, relate those values to the Zone System, raise or lower certain values through adjusted exposure, and allow for expansion or contraction in development of the negative.

Twenty years ago, when I first became aware of the Zone System as a means of exposure and development control, I was quite confused by its approach to photography. The reason I was confused was due to the fact that I had not learned (or taught myself) how to visualize the subject as the final image in my mind's eye. With experience and continued use of the Zone System, visualization and seeing the actual finished print in my mind, became more and more of a reality.

Unlike former means of exposing the negative, the Zone System is not a means of light averaging, nor is it to be associated with bracketing (making numerous negatives of various exposures). In printing, changing to different grades of paper does not fully accomplish the results for which the Zone System was intended. Proper Zone System use is not possible without previsualization of the subject. Most papers today cannot render the extreme low to high values a negative is capable of recording. Zone system photography can bring this wide (or narrow) exposure range within the latitude of the papers capability. An excellent explanation of visualization can be found in Ansel Adams: The Negative, and should be studied thoroughly by the serious student.

The subject here, Calla Lily and Caladium is an example of a limited amount of expansion to the negative.

With Zone 0 being solid black, and Zone I being virtually solid black, I placed the value of the dark green leaves between Zones III/IV (a Zone which assures good definition of the subject values). The white bloom fell between Zones VI/VII–slightly low to create a clean luminous value. To lighten the bloom about 1/2 stop to Zone VII, adding more brilliance as visualized on the ground glass, I indicated Normal-plus-one development. With development expansion, the low values do not rise as fast proportionally as do the higher values above Zone V.

My camera, a 4 x 5 Omega View camera of steel construction, was aligned at about 2 1/2 feet from the bloom. I used Tri-X film (ASA 200). The indicated basic exposure, f 32/45 at 1/4 second, was adjusted to f 22/32 at 1/4 second due to bellows extension. The negative was developed in FG7 (1:15). I have made excellent prints on both Elite and Mitsubishi grade 3 papers developed 1 minute in Selectol Soft (1:1) followed by 2 minutes in Edwal Ultra Black (1:6), or LPD (1:3), and toned in selenium (1:20) for 6 minutes.

I have found it very important to keep good records of film, lenses used, exposure, light readings and other technical data pertaining to the negative and printing of each subject, and call on this information at future times for similar situations.

Corn Lily
Lakewood, California

I had spent the morning outside photographing Calla lilies in the north light by my house. After I had finished and brought all of my equipment inside, I noticed the corn lily in the corner of the room—its leaves translucent in the sunlight. As I draped the dark side of my focusing cloth behind the plant, I visualized the strong design of the leaves.

I set up my 4 x 5 Omega view camera with a 7 1/4-inch Schneider Symmar S lens. I took several readings with my spot meter to determine the placement of the values on the exposure scale. The dark background was placed on Zone III. The brightest edge of the lower corner leaf fell on Zone VII. The middle tones of the upper leaf fell on Zone V. My film at the time was Super XX, one of the still remaining thick emulsion films, manufactured originally for use in color separations for printing purposes. The film, extremely sensitive to all colors of the spectrum, accurately transfers the color hues to black and white, and allows for high degrees of development expansion—more than most current modern day sheet films. An exception to this is the new Ilford HP5+, which, when processed in Pyro PMK or HC-110, produces admirable negatives of fine tones and scale.

Depth of field was a problem, and focus of the leaves near the back was difficult even at f 32/45. I finally decided I could maintain a greater depth of field and a higher degree of sharpness if I moved the camera back about 1 1/2 feet. The image could be cropped in tighter when printing. I made the 1/2 second exposure on Super XX at ASA 200. The negative was deep tank developed in D-25 for 15 minutes with continuous agitation the first

7 minutes, and 30 seconds each minute thereafter. It was then given a second bath in Kodalk for 3 minutes. As expected, the image is cropped in the final printing, eliminating unwanted leaves and lines that distract from the original concept. I found too, that the flopped image on the ground glass was aesthetically more acceptable than the first few test prints, which were printed the way a negative would ordinarily be printed. All prints since have been printed as shown here. Corn Lily has been enlarged up to 20 x 24 and is a relatively easy negative to print. The print is on Elite grade 3 developed 2 minutes in Edwal Ultra Black (1:7) followed by toning in selenium (1:20) for 5 minutes.

Although this photograph was made in the house, I do not consider it contrived, but rather a found subject. Had the subdued sunlight not been shining through the curtains on the leaves at the precise moment, I might have passed over this subject entirely.

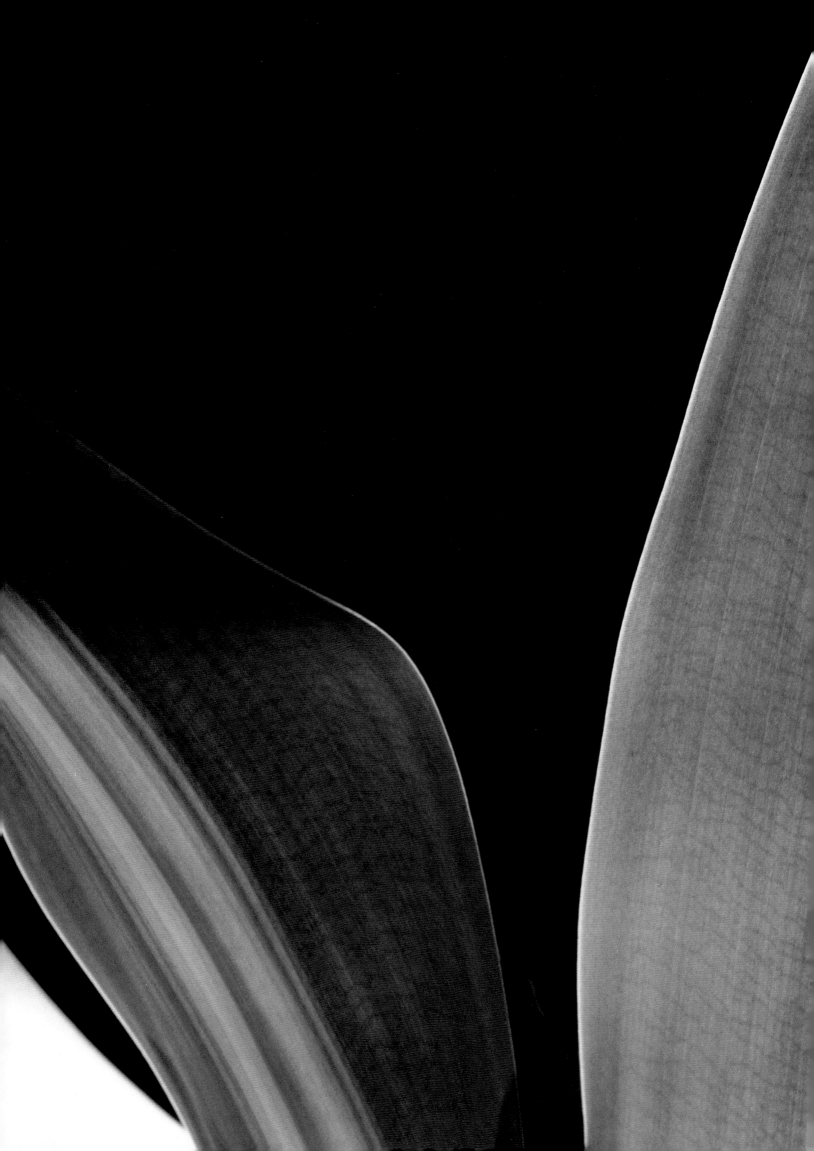

Eggs in a Basket
Lakewood, California

As a gesture of neighborly friendship one Christmas, I was given a woven basket full of jams and pickles. Once empty, the basket had set in front of the fireplace for quite some time. As I looked at it often, I tried to figure it into a photographic composition. By spring the jams and pickles were gone and it contained two large pine cones that I had brought back from one of the Sierra trips.

One day months later, I was figuring an appropriate way to photograph some eggs, when I happened to remember the basket. Filling it with a dozen or more eggs, fifteen to be exact, I took the basket outside and placed it on a large cutting board I had taken from the kitchen. The lighting, as it was from the sun, was too intense, creating harsh lines and strong shadows. I moved everything to the shade, but the subject was flat and dull. With a card, I tried bouncing sunlight onto the subject. I wanted the appearance of soft, warm light shaping the roundness of the eggs. I returned the basket and eggs to the full sun and set up a reflectosol about 3 feet above the eggs, with the subdued sunlight shining through it onto the subject. This lighting was very effective in achieving the desired image. The tripod stood vertically over the basket with the legs at the outer edges of the cutting board. I had to maneuver around in several positions to eliminate any shadows created by the legs.

I used an 8 x 10 ANBA view camera with a 9 1/2-inch Nikkor lens. I had somewhat of a depth of field problem, and would have preferred a shorter lens at the time, but did not have one that would cover the 8 x 10 format. The shorter lens would have also placed me closer to the subject and that could have caused problems with a

shadow from the camera. I took readings with a Pentax spot meter, placing the dark inside bottom of the basket on Zone III, and the highlights of the eggs on Zone V. I made the exposure at f 64 for 1 second on Tri-X 320 (rated at 200). To expand the scale of the subject, I gave Normal-plus-two development in FG7 (1:15) for 27 minutes with agitation the first minute and 15 seconds every two minutes thereafter. I forgot to allow for lens extension in the exposure, so I made another negative at f 64 for 3 seconds, however, the first negative was correct.

The print is on Galerie grade 3 developed in Dektol (1:2) for 2 1/2 minutes, followed by selenium toning for 6 minutes.

Although this is not a found subject, but a contrived one, the print works well for me in expressing the aesthetic qualities of fine art photography.

Onions and Dried Grass
Lakewood, California

One rainy morning I was looking around the house for subjects to photograph. Previously I had photographed Eggs in a Basket, but I was looking for something new. I decided to get in my car and take a drive to a produce market only a few blocks away. I looked over all of the fruit and vegetables. When I saw a bin of onions, an idea developed in my mind's eye. I visualized the final print while I was standing at the produce stand. I selected one-half-dozen onions of similiar shapes and sizes.

Returning back home I headed for the garage. There was a shelf with old tar paper backing that seemed to be the ideal place for the row of onions. I lined up the onions and had one left over, so it was stacked on top of the others. Dried grass had grown through the cracks in the weather-boarding and had spread over the back wall. When I looked in the ground glass the composition was as I had first visualized it. The cloudy weather added soft lighting that spilled in from the outside where the garage door was open. The lighting looked good, but the image was a little too flat. I had an old light socket and found a 150 watt bulb for it. The bulb gave exactly the right amount of light to add a white highlight to the onions, as well as add shape and form, giving them roundness.

My lens on the 4 x 5 view camera was a 3 1/2-inch Schneider Angulon. With my spot meter I took four readings. The dark shaded part of the shelf was placed on Zone III; the background wall fell between Zones III and IV; the shaded side of the onions on Zone V with the highlights between Zones VII/VIII. I used Plus X (ASA 80). The indicated exposure was 1/2 second at f 32. With the 3 1/2-inch lens I was about 18 inches from the subject. Due to the bellows extension, I added one more stop—1 second at f 32. Development was Normal in HC-110 (dilution B) for 5 minutes.

I pulled the dried grass from the shelf and made two more exposures, however, when I made test prints, the latter images lacked the interest and composition of the first one. I have made excellent prints on Galerie, Mitsubishi and Oriental, all grade 3, and most recently on Elite grade 3 developed in Selectol Soft (1:1) for 45 seconds followed by Glycin 130 (1:1) for 2 minutes. The print is toned in selenium (1:20) for 6 minutes.

The image, which works quite well in all sizes up to 20 x 24, has been one of my most popular ones, and is very expressive of black-and-white fine art photography.

Sunrise Through Fog
Point Mugu, California

Land and ocean—certainly two opposing forces—can join together and exhibit one of nature's most profound beauties. Each time these two forces meet there is a sense of tremendous power. Visually, the meeting of land and sea is always different. Light can be striking and cutting, or it can be subdued, subtle or soft.

In the case of this photograph, made just after sunrise one early fall morning, the power of nature's effects is evident. Early, before sunrise, there had been a heavy fog along the coast from Santa Monica to the Ventura County line. As daylight began to break, I looked for areas that might be good prospects for photographs. Light along some of the rocks and beach of the west facing coast was drab and dismal.

I turned the car around near Port Hueneme and headed back toward Pt Mugu State Park. As I was making the bend in the road, I saw the sun rising through the fog over the Santa Monica Mountains. On one hand the scene was quite brilliant, with the light striking the ocean like a silvery blanket—on the other hand, it was soft, with enveloping light falling gently on the dark rocks which accented the gentle surf.

I pulled over, parked the car at cliffs edge and got my camera equipment together for the short hike down the path to the rocks below. Realizing that I might encounter some early morning wind along the coast, I had taken my Mamiya 645 Super. My equipment included three lenses—45, 80 and 210mm—and three film backs with Verichrome 120; one for Normal development, Normal minus and Normal plus.

I set up my tripod and camera in the rocks about thirty feet above the ocean. The waves were pounding heavily, but there was no wind at all to contend with. I had to work fairly fast at this point because the sun was now rising quickly and in a short time it would be out of the composed area.

With my Pentax spotmeter I took a reading of the dark rocks along the oceans edge and placed them on Zone II. The bright sun shining through the fog was placed high on the scale at Zone XI. The gray water of the ocean fell on Zone V, and the highlights of the water on Zone VIII. In order to hold all the information in the fog and clouds around the sun, I indicated N-1 development, with an additional 3 minutes in 1% Kodalk to fully develop the low shadow areas. The negative, containing all of the information of the scene, still requires considerable burn-in at the printing stages in order to fulfill my original visualization and interpretation of the scene. An ordinary straight photograph of this particular subject would be quite flat and rather dull, with considerable loss of detail in the high values. Through visualization, negative development, and image enhancement at the printing stage, I am able to present a photograph of a subject that I saw in my mind's eye which was quite different from the actual scene.

During this particular morning I made numerous photographs of the rocks, surf and ocean at Point Mugu. Each photograph is quite different in its own way due to the ever changing light along the shore. Just as light and shadow change each hour of every day, visualization in photography changes, too.

Dinghy
Long Beach Marina

The making of a fine art photograph involves a great deal more than just having a knowledge of the use of film and paper. It involves the art of visualization, and how a subject is transformed into a photographic piece of art.

I have made an abundance of photographs in the earlier years that turned out very well—others were failures. Those that turned out well, were the ones where I had a strong sense of visualization of the subject, and how I wanted to interpret the scene. Once I see the finished, final photograph in my mind's eye, the entire technique of the making of the negative falls into place.

With visualization, a great amount of time is saved in the darkroom trying to manipulate a negative into the making of a fine art print.

This photograph of Dinghy, Long Beach Marina is a good example of pre-visualization. When I came upon this subject one early summer morning, I immediately saw the final print in my mind. I knew precisely what I must do to interpret the subject and transform the information to the negative. First and foremost, I saw the bright shape of the hull dropping down into the photograph against a dark background. In actuality, the hull was a mauve color, but I visualized it to be bright white, with only a subtle indication of the ribbing on the bottom. The reflection of the boat in the water was dark, accenting the bright shape. And, behind the dark shadow, was the background of deep gray tones, lying at the water's depths like painted textures.

The first thing I did was to check the brightness of the sunlit hull. It was placed on Zone VIII. The dark shadow accenting the boat fell on Zone I/II, and the gray back-ground water on IV/V. To insure a very deep black reflection of the boats shadow, and to assure the holding of some tone in the ribbing on the hull, I placed all of the readings one-half Zone lower on the scale. I photographed this subject on two different 120 films. One exposure was on HP5+ exposed at an ASA of 260, the other on Verichrome at ASA 100. Both negatives are very good, with the Verichrome having a slight edge when it comes to fine grain and detail in the high values. Normal development in PMK Pyro for 9 1/4 minutes gave me extremely sharp and fine grain negatives that enlarge very well to 16x20. This image is relatively easy to print on a number two paper, due to successful pre-exposure visualization of the image. I see this as a quiet photograph which conveys my emotions and feelings at the time of visualization and exposure.

Reflections, Morning Sun
Long Beach, California

Several years ago, when I lived in the Long Beach area of Southern California, I would rise early on many mornings and drive down to the Marina before dawn. I always had at least one camera with me in the hope that I would find new and interesting subjects which would lend themselves to a few negatives.

At certain times of the year the fog can be quite prevalent along the coastal areas. It is on these foggy mornings that the light is very soft and somber, giving subjects almost a fantasy like quality.

With camera in hand, I would walk the docks around the marina enjoying the fresh, brisk air. Except for the taut ropes pulling against the docks, and the creaking of boats shifting in their moorings, it was extremely quiet.

On the morning when I made this image, the sun was just beginning to rise. In the calm waters around the boat slips there were very brilliant reflections that would change and intensify with each minute of the rising sun. Occasionally there would be a ripple caused by the rocking of a boat. This often added interesting effects to a reflected image and created unusual patterns and designs.

I set up my 8x10 view camera on one of the launching docks about 30 feet from the reflections that I wanted to photograph. With a framing card, I carefully composed the image, taking into account the edges and corners of the subject. I determined that a 12-inch lens (300mm) was of the correct focal length to get the exact cropping I wanted. I spent considerable time visualizing this image, and determining in my mind's eye how the values should be placed on the scale and how they would translate to the negative and final print.

In order to obtain the dense blacks that I visualized, the deepest shadows were placed low on the scale on Zone II. The gray water fell on Zone IV and the high values of the sun on the bow of the boat fell on Zone VIII. In order to limit the amount of the rocking movement of the boats, and to eliminate some of the rippling effects of the water, I used a fairly fast shutter speed. I decided at the time of exposure that rating the Tri-X film at ASA 500, and processing the film in Ethol UFG with normal development, would assure the full tonal range and latitude of the film and maintain all of the exposure values of the subject.

The print holds the detail quite well in the high value areas. The extreme highlights, which are right on the threshold, add a certain amount of brilliance to the image. The basic print exposure is 30 seconds on Arista Classic grade 3. Using a card, and working up from the bottom, the water is burned in an additonal 4 seconds to deepen the black in the lower half. The edges and corners also receive an additional 4 second burn. The print is developed in Glycin 130 1:1 for 3 minutes and toned in a selenium/hypo clearing agent combination solution for 5 minutes.

I have always enjoyed looking at reflections in water and find their ever changing compositions very interesting. In this particular image of Reflections, the actual subject above the water line is not nearly as interesting and thought-provoking as the reflection itself of the object in the water. Many times I have returned to this subject, but have never found it to have the same substance and quality of light.

Fence Post Along the Owens River
Owens Valley, California

The Eastern Sierra, although quite desolate on the surface to one visiting for the first time, is a mixture of beautiful scenery and adventure. Many of the remote reaches can be explored in all seasons of the year. Climate and panoramic vistas are constantly changing.

Nestled between the White Mountains to the east, and the cresting Sierra to the west, is the Owens Valley, a beautiful expanse combining desert and lava rock giving evidence of great geological volcanic activity in the past. Alkali flats stretch across its floor.

In summer the desert of the Owens Valley is hot and dry. In winter it is often blanketed by snow from storms crossing the Sierra range. Spring flowers are in abundance, but water is scarce.

The Owens River narrows to a trickle at points, creating a calm and almost mirror-like surface.

One very early morning, before sunrise, I was driving about and came upon a fence running adjacent to the river. The dawn light reflecting from the upper atmosphere enhanced the bleached fence post next to a cove of dry brush. I was fascinated by the textures of the wood, and the design of the subject against the background.

Using my wooden tripod, I set up my field camera with a 7 1/4-inch lens. Upon taking readings with my spotmeter, it was clear that there was about a four-Zone scale to the subject.

Realizing that the use of a green No. 11 filter would lower the reddish values of the brush, and increase contrast of the subject to background, I placed the lowest values of the brush on Zone III. The light yellow brush fell on Zone V, and the post on Zone VI. My film was Tri-X (rated at ASA 260). I indicated Normal plus 1 development to bring the high values of the post up to Zone VII. Anything higher would have resulted in blocking up of the high values, with loss of texture and definition. To assure fine grain and high acutance—strengthening this image both in detail and brilliance—I indicated PMK Pyro developer, which added considerable density to the subject through staining during the fixing and washing process.

The print is on Arista Classic 3 developed in Glycin 130 (diluted 1:1) for 3 minutes. Toning in Selenium at 1:12—with hypo clearing agent—for 6 minutes solidifies the image quite well. To emphasize the brilliance of the post, I do a small amount of dodging during the printing stage to hold back the density, enhancing the separation of the subject to background.

For me this subject is a pleasant one which makes a statement about rather quiet surroundings of this particular area at the time of exposure.

Leaf and Root Patterns
Arcadia, California

As I have done so many times in the past, I arose early in the morning and drove to the Los Angeles County Arboretum in Arcadia. This beautiful and very serene area is hidden from the frantic everyday pace of the metropolitan area of Southern California.

The variety of plant life is endless—from the bamboo trees and ferns of the wet tropics, to the cactus of the dry and desolate deserts of the Southwest.

The jungle setting of the Arboretum was the sight for many years for the Tarzan movies—and in recent years, the Fantasy Island television series.

When a few hours are spent at the Arboretum, one gets the feeling of being away with nature and thoughts of the crowded city vanish. Peacock, swan and ducks, roaming the hills abundant with foliage, dip, dive and dart in the warm waters of the lagoons.

On this particular day my attention was drawn to the old trees, tree trunks and dead stumps, which are numerous along the banks of the lagoons.

This photograph of a very old rubber tree, which I call Leaf and Root Patterns, was made in a very remote, and dark area of the Arboretum. The limited light which filtered through the trees was soft and flat. When I first took the basic readings with my spot meter, there was only a two-stop difference from the low values to the highest values. I say "low to highest", because there really weren't any high values. The scene overall was quite flat with little depth and separation.

I decided at the time that in order to expand the values considerably, I would need to use increased development in Pyro—which, through the yellow

staining of the negative would add the density necessary to produce the desired visualized image.

I set up my 4x5 Wista field camera with a Schneider 180mm lens. My film was Ilford HP5+ (rated at ASA 260), a very fine high speed film with extended tonal range and wonderful grain structure.

With my spot meter, I took readings of the only two values evident in the root patterns. Because of the high expansion of development intended, I placed the low shadows among the roots low on the scale between Zones I/II, the highest values evident fell low on Zone IV/V—Normal plus 2 development in Pyro would raise them to VI/VII, quite satisfactory for high values for a subject such as this. The value of the leaf was actually lower than the brightest part of the roots. I decided to use a yellow K2 filter to accent the leafs shape and help raise its value.

When I saw the negative in the hypo, I was quite pleased with the success of expansion, which increased the densities well. This subject, quite flat in subdued light, expanded well to give a sense of form and depth not found in the original subject. I made a duplicate negative which I developed in HC-110 (dilution B), but the detail, sharpness and overall resolution of the PMK Pyro negative was far superior.

The print is on Arista Classic 2, developed in Glycin 130 with one-fourth the amount of hydroquinone. Toning is in Selenium (with hypo clearing agent) 1:12 for 7 minutes. Arista Classic tones moderately well and intensifies greatly, adding a pronounced depth to the blacks in the print.

Aspens, Lake Lundy
High Sierra

I have made many trips to the Sierra and do not believe there has been a time that was not exciting with aesthetically pleasing results both in winter and in summer. The range to the north can be rich with water-falls and blooming wildflowers in spring, and rustic and somber during fall.

Numerous photographic compositions are evident once we seek out the qualities of the surrounding environment. If the photographer knows his craft well, he is able to interpret the compositions and respond to them appropriately, turning them into images of the expressive moment.

On this trip I spent several days hiking about, photo-graphing along the shores of Grant, Gull and June Lakes. The altitude is 9500 feet and the air crisp and clear on October days. The sun was warm and bright for the most part. I had been as far north as Bridgeport and Twin Lakes, and had now returned to the Lake Lundy area in the Inyo National Forest.

Driving west along the old lake road, I came upon a beautiful aspen grove, back-lighted in the mid-morning sun. The tall, dry summer grass surrounded the trees, already somewhat stripped of their golden leaves by falls embrace. There was a slight breeze coming off the lake as I set up my tripod and 8 x 10 field camera with a 9 1/2-inch Nikkor lens. There was a softness of light and a short scale, evident by the meter readings. The dark shaded areas and ground shadows were placed on Zone IV, knowing some of the smaller tree limbs and edges along the shaded side of the trunks would fall lower. I wanted to make sure there were no other large

harsh areas of solid black. The tree and background highlights fell between Zones VI/VII, only a 2 1/2 stop luminance range, quite short on the photographic scale. The yellow K2 filter I used lightened the highlights of both the turning leaves and dry grass, and lowered the shadows closer to Zone III. The adjusted exposure after the filter factor of one was 1/4 second at f 32. I indi-cated Normal-plus-two development of the Tri-X (ASA 200) film in HC-110 (dilution B).

I find this image very expressive of the scene, not as it was at the time of exposure, but as I visualized it in my mind's eye. I have made prints on Agfa Brovira, Oriental Seagull, Galerie, Elite and Mitsubishi, all grade 3, from 8 x 10 to 30 x 40. The image holds up extremely well in all sizes. If I had not taken the time to visualize the final image, I feel this subject would have turned out drab and flat—a good reason to plan each step well before the actual exposure is made.

GLOSSARY

ASA Exposure Index–The ASA stands for American Standard Association...a method of film speed rating, and which has, since 1943, become the standard used by all exposure meter, film, strobe and flash manufacturers.

Acetic Acid–A weak acid used for compounding short stops. Has a strong odor. Used in acidifying fixing baths and in short stop baths.

Adjustments–Using swings and tilts to the front and rear standards of a view camera to align perspective and to bring subjects or portions of subjects into proper focus.

Adjusted Exposure–The increase or decrease of exposure due to bellows extension, or the use of filters. Long exposures resulting in reciprocity effects require adjusted exposures.

Citric Acid–A tribasic organic acid used as a preservative in developers–also as the acid constituent in some fixing and clearing baths.

Acutance–The objective means of measuring a photographic film which shows a sharp line of separation between adjoining areas receiving different exposure. Acutance is referred to many times as the edge sharpness within the image.

Agitation–The movement of film and paper in the various photographic solutions during processing. Agitation most commonly is done by hand or by rocking the trays. A consistent means of agitation is important to accomplish even development.

Anastigmat–A type of photographic lens from which all astigmatism errors have been removed. All high quality and professional lenses for 35mm cameras up to large format are most often anastigmat.

Antifoggant–A chemical which is added to developing solutions to inhibit fogging of sensitized photographic film and paper, due to outdated materials, extended developing, or when safelights are too intense.

Bellows–The folding body extension of a view camera or enlarger, usually made of leather or cloth. Contracts in folds as the lens is moved in or out during focusing.

Bellows Extension–The degree to which a bellows will extend. The shorter the lens, the less extension; a long lens requires a very extended bellows; as well as subjects which are extremely close to the lens. Long bellows extensions require longer adjusted exposures due to the distance of light travel from lens to the film plane.

Blocking up–A term used to indicate areas of a negative which contain no detail due to the loss of density caused by over-exposure and/or over development.

Boric Acid–Used in fixing baths. Has a hardening property which helps prevent sludge on films.

Bracketing–The making of a number of exposures above and below the indicated exposure of a meter, usually at increments of one f/stop at time.

Brilliance–In a lens, the ratio of transmitted light to incident light. All lenses transmit light to different degrees. Two lenses set at the same f/stop may require different exposures due to brilliance.

Bromide Emulsion–An emulsion of silver bromide and gelatin which is used as the sensitive coating of photographic papers. Bromide emulsion is much faster in the enlarging process as compared to silver bromide used for contact printing.

Burning In–A means of controlling tones in a photographic print by using a card to burn in edges of a print to darken, or a card with a hole in it, whereby only a small amount of light is permitted to be exposed on the paper.

Camera, View–A commercial camera used for professional purposes in both the studio and out in field. Also referred to as a field camera, however the structures are somewhat different. View cameras are usually on a monorail of which the front and rear standards move from front to back. A field camera folds in a more compact fashion. The view and field have many adjustments for focus and perspective and can accommodate a large variety of lenses.

Carbonate–Salts formed by the combination of some metal with carbon. In photography, the most common is sodium carbonate.

Chalky–The extreme harshness or hard contrast of a print in which the highlights are pure white with poor or no detail whatsoever.

Changing Bag–A large bag, usually black, made of a number of thicknesses of material, with holes for arms to enter. Used for loading and unloading film in small cameras, and for loading film holders out in the field, on location, when no darkroom is available.

Chloride Paper–Very slow printing paper for contact prints. Emulsion contains primarily chloride of silver.

Chlorobromide–A type of printing paper which gives warm, black tones. It is the intermediate between chloride and bromide papers.

Closeup–The tightness by which a subject is cropped–when only a portion is framed in the viewfinder or on the ground glass of a view camera. Moving the camera in on the subject, isolation of the subject. A bouquet of flowers could be considered a medium composition, moving in on one flower or bloom would be a closeup.

Condenser, Optical–An enlarging system in which lenses intercept a comparatively large cone of light rays emitted by a source such as a lamp or blub. These rays are concentrated within a specified area. The condenser light system is used on a much more limited basis than in years past, when it was the primary form of projection enlarging of the negative. Recent times have seen the more efficient cold light as the preferred light source, due mainly to its low heat and high quality, eliminating imperfections in the negative.

Contact Paper–A chloride coated photographic paper, which is printed by keeping it in direct contact with the negative during exposure in a frame on

102

either the enlarger baseboard, or a separate printing frame held under some other light source.

Contact Printing–To expose paper in contact with the negative, as opposed to projection in an enlarger.

Contraction Development–The reduction of contrast to the film negative, bringing the tonal values of an extremely bright scene to within the desired printable range as visualized at the time of exposure. Selected tones of the gray scale may be contracted as necessary to change the overall concept. Contraction should not be confused with under development. Reduced development indicates the need for more exposure–one half to as much as two stops more–depending on the degree of contraction.

Contrast–The degree of difference between the darkest tones and the lightest ones on the photographic scale–on both film and paper.

Contrast Grades–The range of tones available in the photographic paper emulsions. A contrast grade is matched to the density of the negative. Paper grades run from No. 0 to No. 5 or 6. A high contrast negative would print on one of the lower numbered grades–a low contrast negative would require a higher number. No. 2 and 3 are considered the average, and are the most common paper grades used.

Crop–The trimming of a print to include only the desired area. Cropping can also be done in the camera on the ground glass by moving the camera closer or further from the subject, or by changing to a shorter or longer focal length lens.

Daguerreotype–The first photograph. A thin, negative image on a silver plate appears as a positive by means of reflected light. A silver plate is sensitized by fuming with iodine, then developing with mercury vapor after making the exposure.

Dark Slide–The protective slide which covers the film in the film holder when not in the camera. The Dark Slide is pulled out after the seating of the holder in the camera. Once the exposure is made, the slide is replaced before removing the film holder.

Density–The amount of silver that is deposited in a given area on film and paper. The amount of light which will pass through the silver. A negative or print that is flat and lifeless will consist of low density and be unpleasing to the eye.

Depth of Field–The distance between two points that contains a sharp image. The smaller the f/stop the greater this distance. A lens that is wide open will have a shallow depth of field.

Developer–The chemical or solution which causes development. When light strikes a sensitive emulsion a change takes place in the silver halide. This change makes it possible to remove the bromine from the exposed portions of silver bromide by chemical reduction. There are literally dozens of commonly used developers for both film and paper. The most common, though, of all of these is Dektol for paper. Many contain metol (Elon) or Phenidone. Borax developer is an accelerator developer which is known for its medium grain and superb gradation.

Diffusion–An additional screen or filtration used over the lenses of cameras or enlargers to produce softer definition of the subject. Sometimes used in the printing of portraits to eliminate unwanted facial lines or wrinkles. Extreme diffusion in the enlarger can create beautiful effects, creating subjects with a hazy softness.

Dodging–The procedure of holding back the light from the enlarger on a certain portion of the projected image. Wires with small discs on the ends are used to move over a small part of the image, lightening that area. On the edges of large prints, the hand can be used to hold back light.

Emulsion–The mixture of sensitive silver salts and gelatin on film and paper. The light sensitive area of photographic materials.

Emulsion Speed–The sensitometric measurement of an emulsion's ability to produce a certain density with controlled exposure conditions. Speeds can vary greatly from as slow (ASA 9) to tremendously fast films (ASA 6400). The more common emulsion speeds are ASA 125 to 400.

Enlarger– A projector able to cast the image of a negative onto a piece of photographic paper for the exposure.

Etching–The scraping away of small unwanted spots on a print. The removal, or lightening of a portion of a negatives emulsion to reduce density by means of etching chemicals.

Exhibition–The display of a body of photographic work in a gallery or museum.

Exhibition Mount–The white mounting board which a print is affixed to before matting or framing. All photographic prints should be mounted on 100% rag board to assure permanency.

Expansion Development–Increasing development of a low value, low luminance scene to render it printable on the photographic paper as visualized at the time of exposure. Expanded development requires less exposure from one to as much as two f/stops. Expansion raises selected values from the mid to highlight range. Lower zones around I, II, and III are less effected by expanded development than the higher values. Super XX, one of the few remaining thick emulsion films will allow as much as a four or five zone increase. Considerable grain is evident with newer films of recent decades, which do not allow long developing times.

Exposure–The making of a photographic print by exposing the sensitive paper to the projected light from the enlarger, or by contact printing. The definite light action on the film resulting from the time the shutter remains open on the camera and the f/stop used.

Exposure Factor–Any adjustment to the exposure of a negative due to the use of filters, light intensity, shutter speed or f/stop.

Exposure Meter–The light meter is used to measure the intensity of light from a subject. The light can be measured as reflected light from the scene or incident light which is measured as the light actually falling directly on the subject. The professional photographer finds the measurement of light to be so critical that a spot meter is invaluable. The spot meter measures 1° of the reflected light in the scene. Numerous readings can be taken of a subject varying from solid black to pure white in both color and black and white photography.

f/ Number–The numerical values of the effective aperture of the lens. These f/ numbers are fractional focal lengths.

Film–A roll or sheet of celluloid used as a base for holding gelatin and silver sensitive photographic material.

Film Holder–A light-proof casing to hold sheet film which is used in view cameras.

Film Pack–A pack usually contains 16 sheets of cut film. Film is arranged so that each exposed piece of film is pulled to the rear of the package after exposure, allowing for a new sheet in front. The film pack has a dark slide to cover the surface of the film, and is removed just before exposure, then replaced immediately thereafter.

Filters–Glass gels used to exaggerate or dramatize the tonal values or colors in a scene. In black and white photography, yellow, green, orange and red are the most used to add depth and separation to a landscape.

Filter UV–A filter which absorbs the ultra-violet but allows all of the visible light to be transmitted by the lens. This filter greatly reduces haze and bluish cast.

Filter Factor–The number of times exposure must be increased due to the use of various filters. The available light is reduced when a filter is used therefore requiring an increase of light from the subject or landscape. Emulsion reacts differently to some light than others. A No. 11 green filter calls for an increase of two stops, where a No. 29 red requires more than a four stop increase. A filter factor of 2x would require opening the lens one more stop. A factor of 8x would require 3 more stops.

Fixing Bath–A solution used for dissolving the unexposed silver halides and the removal of residual sensitive silver from a developed film or print, thereby rendering the image permanent. Also known as hypo, it contains a preservative such as sodium sulphite, acetic acid and a hardening agent.

Focal Length–The distance from the optical center of a lens to its focal point. The focal length may be assumed to be the distance between the ground glass or film plane, and the lens aperture when the lens is focused on infinity.

Focus–The moving of a lens back and forth to bring a subject to sharpness on the ground glass or in the view finder. The meeting point of the light rays as they pass through the lens is the exact point of focus.

Focus, Long focal length–The long distance of the glass from the front to rear of the lens. A telephoto lens.

Focus, Short focal length–A wide angle lens. The short distance of the front and rear elements of the lens.

Focusing Cloth–A large piece of material, usually white on one side, black on the other, to shield the photographer from outside light while composing and focusing a subject on the view camera ground glass.

Focusing Magnifier–A magnifying glass used for examining the image on the ground glass to insure sharp focus.

Fog–Silver deposits becoming visible in parts of the image where they should not appear. Fog can be due to light leaks in the camera bellows or film holder. The most common problem with fog results in the darkroom from inadequate safelights, outdated paper or overused developer. Fog can suppress a photographic image to where the whites become dead and lifeless in a print. Potassium Bromide and Benzotriazole can be added to reduce the chance of fog and brighten high values.

Format–Relating to the size of the film used in the camera or the opening of the aperture. 4 x 5 and 8 x 10 are referred to as large format cameras.

Gelatin–Used in the photographic process to hold the sensitive silver salts. It is similar to glue in being able to harden when cold and become soft when submerged in too warm of developer.

Glass, Ground–The back frosted, rough glass used on a view camera to focus the image projected by the lens.

Grain–Individual silver grains clumped together in varying degrees. Grain sizes vary with different photographic emulsions. Some developers will give finer grain structure than others due to chemical make up and the length of time the film is subjected to the solution.

Gram–A unit of metric weight measurement.

Hydroquinone–One of the more common slow-working developing agents.

Hypo Eliminator–A chemical used to neutralize the hypo from photographic films and papers cutting washing time considerably.

Image–The reproduction of a subject on a photographic material by a lens. An image in the mind's eye may be entirely different from the actual scene before us.

Infinity–An infinite distance. The farthest distance at which a lens focuses.

Intensification–The process by which the silver image is increased to add density, and contrast when development is increased. Intensification in selenium can increase the density of a negative by as much as 1 to 1 1/2 Zones with no increase in grain structure. This is valuable in improving soft negatives which may have previously been considered of little value.

Kodalk–An alkali sometimes used in developing formulas as a replacement for carbonate. Has the ability to be able to control the quantity of alkali more precisely than carbonate. With carbonate developers, small changes in the quantity can greatly alter the activity of the developer. Small changes in Kodalk developers produce very slight changes in the developer activity.

Lens, Coated–Surfaces are specially coated to reduce surface reflections and flairs, and decreases light loss thereby increasing the speed of the lens.

Light Polarization–The Polarizing filter eliminates some of the reflections and glare by controlling waves of light vibrations. The lower the sun is to the horizon, or the various angles we are to the sun, the better the polarized effect will be. At high noon there is virtually no effect at all. Brilliant storm and cloud effects can be achieved with a polarizing filter in conjunction with a yellow or red filter. Even in black and white photography there is increased tonal saturation. With color photography the spectrum of colors can be greatly enhanced adding superb color saturation.

Liter–A unit of liquid measure in the metric system consisting of 1000 milliliters.

Luminance–The measure of the brightness of a luminous surface. Many times luminance is measured in candles-per-square-foot.

Metol–One of best known and most popular of the developing agents. Also known as Elon, metol can be used alone, but most commonly in conjunction with hydroquinone and pyro. A phenidone developer gives practically the same results as a metol developer, and is a non-irritant to the skin.

Newton Rings–A malfunction that happens in the glass negative carrier, or in a contact printing frame whereby concentric circles appear on the final print. These rings, or circles, are caused by light interference patterns created by over-heating, changes in humidity, high pressure between the two pieces of glass, or printing when a negative is not absolutely dry. Sometimes they are hard to eliminate, but for enlarger projection, the cutting of a thin mask out of paper where the negative will rest in the center, can relieve the pressure.

PMK—Pyro Film Developer—An excellent new formula of the '90s developed by Gordon Hutchings. PMK (Pyro, Metol, Kodalk) gives fine grain and sharpness with high acutance. It's staining effect adds printing density to most of today's current films. It is highly concentrate and stock has a long shelf life.

Panchromatic–An emulsion which is sensitive to all visual color–applied to film, and sometimes filters and light sources. Orthochromatic film is sensitive only to ultraviolet, violet, blue and green. Objects which are red are rendered dark or black in the final print.

Paper, Photographic–The paper on which a coating of photographic emulsion is applied for the purpose of making prints from a negative.

Penumbra–The soft edge of a shadow as on the earth when photographed from space. In dodging or burning with a card, the penumbra is at the point on the print where the light shines over the edge of the card, close to the lens to eliminate a sharp or harsh line.

Perspective–The relative size and shape of objects as recorded on a plane surface. The reproduction of a three dimensional subject on a single or flat plane giving the illusion of depth.

Photograph–A reproduction of a scene, object or person on an emulsified film negative from which the image is projected, or made in contact with, on a photographic paper treated with a light sensitive emulsion.

Polaroid–A transparent material containing embedded crystals capable of polarizing light. A Polaroid camera, or a back attachment for view cameras, develops the film negative internally and produces a print, and/or a film negative, within seconds after the process is initiated.

Potassium Bromide–Crystals used in the making of emulsion. Used as a restrainer in developers for both film and paper. Prevents fogging during the developing of prints.

Potassium Carbonate–Can be used as an accelerator instead of sodium carbonate.

Potassium Ferricyanide–Used principally in the hypo-ferricyanide reducer and as a bleach in sulphide toning processes.

Pyro Film Developer–The ABC three part formula, is an excellent fine grain, high acutance developer which gives an appropriate amount of stain, adding density to the image at the time of printing. When handled properly, pyro excels in sharpness and high value resolution with many of the current films on the market today. Extremely toxic, pyro must be dealt with using rubber gloves in a ventilated environment.

Reciprocity Law–The statement that when the illumination of a subject is decreased, a proportionate increase in exposure time will produce an image of the same density. When exposure times are greatly increased, a considerably greater than proportionate increase in time is necessary to maintain the same density.

Reducing Back–A camera back that takes smaller film holders than those for which the camera was originally designed.

Restrainer–The retardation of developer solutions. Bromides and chlorides–namely potassium bromide and benzotriazole–act as anti-foggants and restrain the high values in film and print developing.

Safelight–A light of such color that it will not fog photographic sensitive paper during printing and processing. It is extremely important that the correct safelight is used at all times. Depression of the high values can occur, causing dull and lifeless prints.

Short Stop–An acid bath which immediately stops the development of the negative or print.

Shutter–An apparatus which keeps light from falling upon the emulsion of a film except during the time interval when it is tripped by cable release for the exposure. Can be set at various speeds.

Silver Bromide–The common sensitive salt of emulsions, used either alone or with iodide or chloride.

Spot Meter–A reflected light meter capable of measuring a 1° luminance of a subject.

Stock Solution–A highly concentrated solution of developer which is diluted with water in varying proportions just before use.

Toning–The changing of the tone and the strengthening of the deeper tonal values in a final print. The most widely used is selenium, which gives excellent results on almost all photographic papers. Selenium is usually diluted to 1:12 or 1:20 for use, with prints submerged from 2 to 10 minutes with agitation. Highly concentrated selenium (1:1) is very useful in expanding the contrast and separation within a negative.

Tray Developing–Processing of film and papers in open trays. Especially convenient and clean working for film developing.

Tripod–A three legged support for a camera, usually with adjustable legs to varying lengths. Tripods are fitted with a head that will rotate and tilt at unlimited degrees.

Visualization–The process of seeing in the mind's eye the finished photographic print and how the values will transfer to the print. Proper visualization, and calculating exposure and development are absolute necessities when it comes to Zone System photography.

Washing–One of the most important steps in both film and paper development. Washing removes remaining chemicals from photographic layers within the gelatin surface. Hypo salts must be removed completely in order to make the print permanent and free from discoloration.

Water-Bath Developing–The process of developing the film negative in a solution for a given amount of time, then transferring it to a tray of plain water, whereby the tonal values of the shadows will continue to develop after the developer in the high values has been exasted. It is possible to repeat the steps of transferring the negative back and forth between the developer and the water a number of times.

Zone System–The Zone System approach to black and white photography allows us to move from a very realistic concept to our own personalized interpretation of a subject, and how it will be rendered as a fine print. The technical objective is to establish relationships between various tones. In the Zone System, the darkest tone is Zone 0 (solid black) to Zone X (pure white). Zones are moved higher or lower on the gray scale through adjusted exposure and development. Previsualization and the Zone System go hand-in-hand in allowing us to assign selected tonal values to each part of an image at the moment of exposure. The Zone System should not be confused with bracketing (the making of several exposures at consecutive f/stops above and below a normal reading). By proper application of the Zone System, through exposure adjustments in conjunction with expanded or contracted development, we are able to raise or lower certain, or selected values in the gray scale, producing the desired result.

Sycamore Detail